The Lake of Learning

Also from Steve Berry

Cotton Malone Novels
The Lost Order
The 14th Colony
The Patriot Threat
The Lincoln Myth
The King's Deception
The Jefferson Key
The Emperor's Tomb
The Paris Vendetta
The Charlemagne Pursuit
The Venetian Betrayal
The Alexandria Link
The Templar Legacy
The Bishop's Pawn
The Malta Exchange

Stand-alone Novels
The Columbus Affair
The Third Secret
The Romanov Prophecy
The Amber Room

Steve Berry and M.J. Rose
The Museum of Mysteries

Also from M.J. Rose

Tiffany Blues
The Library of Light and Shadow
The Secret Language of Stones
The Witch of Painted Sorrows
The Collector of Dying Breaths
The Seduction of Victor H.
The Book of Lost Fragrances
The Hypnotist
The Memoirist
The Reincarnationist
Lip Service
In Fidelity
Flesh Tones
Sheet Music
The Halo Effect
The Delilah Complex
The Venus Fix
Lying in Bed

M.J. Rose and Steve Berry
The Museum of Mysteries

The Lake of Learning

A Cassiopeia Vitt Adventure

By M.J. Rose and Steve Berry

EVIL EYE
CONCEPTS

The Lake of Learning
A Cassiopeia Vitt Adventure
By Steve Berry and M.J. Rose

Copyright 2019 Steve Berry and M.J. Rose
ISBN: 978-1-970077-46-9

Published by Evil Eye Concepts, Incorporated

This is a work of fiction. Names, places, characters and incidents are the product of the author's imagination and are fictitious. Any resemblance to actual persons, living or dead, events or establishments is solely coincidental.

Al cap dels sèt cent ans, verdajara lo laurèl.
(The laurel will flourish again in 700 years)

Guilhèm Belibaste
(The last Cathar *Perfecti*,
burned at the stake in 1321)

Chapter 1

Givors, France
Monday, May 4
The Present
11:40 a.m.

Cassiopeia Vitt knew they'd found something important.

How?

Hard to say. Just an instinct that came from years of digging in the dirt, building a castle. It was her labor of love, one that would probably consume her entire adult life. But it was worth it. Especially at moments like this when the French soil finally yielded up its secrets.

"It's definitely something," Viktor said.

A dozen men and women who'd also been working at the construction site had stopped, now gathered around where she and her site superintendent stood. Viktor had been digging an exploratory trench for a new masonry wall that was scheduled to be erected next week when he hit something. The stone for it was being quarried and already rose in piles nearby. She knelt down in the muck and peered into the trench, damp from a rainstorm last night. Despite a thin film of mud, a gleam suggested precious metal.

"Looks like gold," Viktor said.

"Any idea what it is?" she asked.

"From less than an inch exposed?" He laughed. "No idea. There's only one way to find out. Let me dig some more."

"I'll help, it'll go faster."

"Because goodness knows patience isn't one of your best virtues."

"Or yours," she teased back.

She'd been working the project for a long time. Best estimate was that the castle stood at about thirty percent complete. Three curtain walls were up, the fourth still on the drawing board. Several inner buildings had likewise been erected, their interiors though still being planned.

And Viktor was right.

Patience was not her virtue.

Together, they lay flat on their stomachs and carefully set about enlarging the find, slow and careful, using all of the proper techniques to keep it uncorrupted. Painstakingly, trowel by trowel, they removed layers of clay, rock, and debris. Finally, they exposed a corner and enough of one side to see that they'd located a gold box.

"*Ingénieur*, it looks like you've got yourself a treasure chest," Viktor said.

The staff had bestowed upon her the label of engineer during the first year of the project and, while she was generally averse to nicknames, she liked that one.

"Judging by what we can see, I'd say it's about forty-six centimeters wide and about the same in height," she said.

"And with that deduction I suggest we take a break. My back is killing me," Viktor said.

Reluctantly, she agreed. Her own spine also ached from lying on her stomach too long. Yes, she was curious to uncover more. But like Viktor had noted earlier, patience seemed in order.

They left the site and headed toward the high barn that housed the reception center, there to accommodate the several thousand visitors who came every year. Inside, in the back, was an employee kitchen where Cassiopeia brewed them both espressos. Viktor sipped his. She finished hers in two gulps.

"Ready to get back to work and see if we can remove it?" she asked as she laid the cup in the sink.

"Slow down. I said a break not a breath."

She couldn't sit still, so she brewed herself a second coffee.

"I'm as curious as you are," Viktor said. "But that thing has been there a long time. It's not going anywhere. Drink your coffee."

She knew he was right, but it was hard to tamp down her excitement.

Finding artifacts was not unusual. Through the centuries the locale had played host to a variety of historical buildings, starting with a Roman fortress nearly two thousand years ago. Hundreds of items had been unearthed. Things like a 15th century ceramic jug without a chip. A pewter cape closure with a roughhewn topaz at its center. A thick brown glass bottle still containing dregs of ancient olive oil. And, really cool, a sword, maybe 13th century, in a badly deteriorated leather scabbard. All were important and valuable finds, and she planned on displaying them in a museum that would occupy part of the finished castle one day.

So what had the earth yielded this time?

Givors was an ancient place that evolved into an important medieval enclave. Its teardrop-shaped center was still entered through two 14th century gates, designed far more for decoration than defense. Two unremarkable churches lined the main square, along with old houses of wood and stone, the majority now filled with cafés and shops. Most of its inhabitants now lived in the forests beyond. Her chateau was one of many constructed in the 16th century, lovingly maintained through a succession of dedicated owners. Her castle reconstruction project was aimed at reviving one of the region's oldest fortresses, a ruin until she purchased the site and started her project.

The placard near the parking lot that greeted visitors said it all.

WELCOME TO THE PAST. HERE AT GIVORS, A SITE ONCE OCCUPIED BY LOUIS IX, A CASTLE IS BEING CONSTRUCTED USING MATERIALS AND TECHNIQUES ONLY AVAILABLE TO 13TH CENTURY CRAFTSMEN. A MASONED TOWER WAS THE VERY SYMBOL OF A LORD'S POWER. THE CASTLE AT GIVORS WAS DESIGNED AS A MILITARY FORTRESS WITH THICK WALLS AND CORNER TOWERS. THE SURROUNDING ENVIRONS PROVIDED AN ABUNDANCE OF WATER, STONE, EARTH, SAND, AND WOOD, WHICH WERE ALL NEEDED FOR ITS CONSTRUCTION. QUARRIERS, STONE HEWERS, MASONS, CARPENTERS, BLACKSMITHS, AND POTTERS ARE NOW LABORING, LIVING AND DRESSING EXACTLY AS THEY WOULD HAVE EIGHT CENTURIES AGO. THE PROJECT IS PRIVATELY FUNDED AND THE CURRENT ESTIMATE IS

20 YEARS WILL BE NEEDED TO COMPLETE THE
CASTLE. ENJOY YOUR TIME IN THE 13TH CENTURY.

She and Viktor walked back toward the east curtain wall. Overhead loomed a cloudless sky, the warm May air freshened by a floral breeze. Back on their stomachs, they resumed excavation. A half hour of meticulous work revealed a few more centimeters of the box.

"This is a bigger chest than I first thought," Viktor said.

"*You* made a mistake?" Cassiopeia teased.

It was a running joke between them that Viktor was never wrong and, even when he was, he never admitted it. Instead, it was the *circumstances* that had fooled him. Or someone else screwed up? Or, her personal favorite, the whole thing was *a cruel and vicious lie put out by his enemies to discredit him.*

She liked Viktor. They'd attended university together, both working on architectural degrees, hers with a specialty in medieval history. During their second year she'd shared her dream of rebuilding a medieval castle, and that she had the means to make it happen. Five years after they graduated, she asked him to come on board and he'd agreed.

They made a good team.

She produced the initial designs and Viktor changed them. Which was fine, since all of his edits were right on target. She could not have undertaken such a gargantuan project without him. She employed more than 120 men and women who worked year round. The costs were enormous. Luckily her parents had left her a fortune thanks to her Spanish grandfather who, in the 1920s, bought coal, minerals, precious metals, gems, and gold mines all over the world. Today, that output was used in everything from high-end electronics to parts for planes and missiles. Demand never seemed to cease. Since her parents died, the people who ran the corporation had doubled its net worth. She was proud that she was putting some of that capital to historical use.

History should be seen.

Her father taught her that.

She often wished she could show him the site. He'd be so proud. She missed him. They'd been incredibly close. And so similar. Except when it came to religion. Their battles on that subject had been epic, threatening their entire relationship. Her parents were devout Mormons, but she'd never been able to share their beliefs. And not for any hostility oward the Latter-day Saints, who were good people, she just possessed no faith. And God, if he even existed, surely would not have approved of parents and children fighting over believing in Him. She'd never been able to reconcile that her father, brilliant in so many ways, was somewhat irrational when it came to religion. His greatest flaw. His only, in her opinion. He'd firmly believed a divine plan existed that every person had to follow. If done, you were rewarded with heaven and all of its wonders. If you failed, only darkness came your way. For a daughter who idolized her father, his blind faith had been hard to accept. To her, no plan existed. No heaven or hell. The Bible? Just a story made up by men in order to get other men to obey. Religion seemed the last vestige of man's intellectual infancy. A remnant from the past.

Like her castle.

She stared at the find in the ground.

They'd exposed the entire box.

Which had a majesty about it. Definitely gold. The top decorated with an assortment of cabochon stones in the shape of a curious cross, its points dotted. Like an inverted Maltese cross, but shorter and squatter.

"It's the Cross of Toulouse," she said.

She knew the history. First seen in the late 12th century when the counts of Toulouse added the cross to their coat of arms. Eventually, it became the symbol of Languedoc resistance to French invaders during the Albigensian crusades against the Cathars. Today it was called the Occitan cross and sometimes, mistakenly, the Cathar cross.

"Let's see what we have here," Viktor said as he snaked ropes underneath the chest.

She helped, then they each grabbed the ends and lifted.

"This is heavy," Viktor said as they struggled.

Finally, they freed the chest from its grave and settled it on the ground.

She immediately snapped a dozen pictures from every angle with a high-resolution camera.

The entire work crew had gathered around, the excitement among them palpable. It was that way with every find. Thankfully, no paying visitors were around today. The site was closed on Mondays to allow for some of the heavy lifting to happen without the worry of hurting anyone. Shelby Randall, a journalist embedded at the site for the past week, there to write a piece about the castle for the magazine *Archéologie*, swept in and snapped some pictures of her own.

"You do the honors, *Ingénieur*," Viktor said.

She brushed the remaining mud off the lid in soft, easy strokes. Viktor leaned forward and together they inspected the container.

"Definitely gold," Viktor said. "It had to come from a church or cathedral."

She agreed. "It looks like they melted some wax and created an airtight seal all the way around the lid."

Which meant there could be something quite valuable inside. Given the style, ornamentation, and materials it appeared like some sort of religious casket.

"I'd bet those are gem quality cabochon rubies embedded in the design," she said.

"If there are rubies on the outside, what's inside?" Shelby Randall asked.

Good question.

Cassiopeia reached out and stroked the latch, then hesitated, savoring the anticipation. Shelby inched closer, ready for the reveal shot. Cassiopeia lifted the latch, opened the lid, and peered into the box. Inside, an object lay wrapped in a gray silk fabric, eaten by time but still relatively intact.

She fingered the tattered cloth. "It's silk."

"And it survived," Viktor said, "thanks to the seal."

She lifted the object out, freeing it from the casket. How long had it lain there? Hard to say at this point. Best guess? Given the Occitan cross, sometime in the past eight hundred years. Which wasn't saying much.

She laid the object on the ground and parted the moldy silk.

Revealing a book.

Its binding fashioned of a tooled, dark brown leather. About twenty centimeters tall and twelve wide. In the center of the front cover lay a raised medallion consisting of two gilt concentric circles enclosing a stylized rose that glowed red and purple in the late morning sun. It reminded her of Notre Dame's famous rose window in miniature. Dozens of chipped rubies and amethyst stones were set into the leather to create a startling resemblance. The top and bottom outer corners were covered with gold protectors and, in the middle of the right edge, a gold clasp held the pages together. Staining of the edges evidenced moisture damage.

"When would you date it?" she asked Viktor, interested in his opinion.

"Thirteenth to 14th century, based on the decoration," he said, pointing at the cover. "But the outside can be quite different from inside. The cover could have been reused."

She agreed.

They'd seen that before.

She carefully undid the clasp and opened the book to reveal an illuminated manuscript. They were all stunned by the quality of the work, riveted by its beauty and rarity. On the title page were the words *Libre de las Õras,* Book of Hours, in Occitan.

"That's odd," she said. "Not Latin."

Viktor nodded. "That is unusual."

The pages were highly illustrated with the anthropomorphic initials of monks, most likely the artists themselves. The indigos, emeralds, and crimsons seemed as resplendent as if they'd been painted yesterday. Every letter, finished in chrysography—a mix of powdered gold and gum—glowed in the sunlight.

She slowly turned the page.

A braid, painted in gold and silver, bordered on the right and left. The left braid enclosed an elaborate figurative biblical scene, still clear, untouched by time. On the right historiated letters, with an illustration inside, led off a block of text. Every millimeter of white space was filled with complex floral motifs utilizing silver and gold, along with more blues, greens, and reds. She turned to another equally magnificent page, rich with designs that the eye could not resist.

"Illuminated manuscripts of this quality are rare," she said.

Viktor nodded. "Tell me about it. This one is a beauty."

Shelby, at Cassiopeia's elbow, clicked away, her camera recording each reveal. The sound caught Cassiopeia's attention and brought her back to reality.

"Okay, show's over," she said. "We need to get this inside and sealed away. The middle of a construction site isn't the best place to study such a precious find. And all of you need to get back to work."

The crowd dispersed and she and Viktor rewrapped the book.

"My father would have loved this," she said.

"Something else he collected?" Viktor asked.

She smiled. "Sometimes I think he had no choice but to become successful, just to indulge his passion for art."

"Lucky man that he was a billionaire."

"He was nothing if not determined and disciplined. He had a great interest in hand-painted religious tomes. He admired monks who lived in isolation, hunched over their desks in scriptoria. I think he was a little jealous of them."

"Jealous?"

"They had a freedom in their isolation that he never enjoyed. The time needed to create infinite beauty. As he called it."

Illuminated manuscripts were the picture books, the coffee-table books, of the Middle Ages. Hard to produce and expensive. Reserved for special texts, like a Bible. Or, like here, a Book of Hours, which noted prayers appropriate for different times in the liturgical day. Many of the wealthy possessed such a book. They were mainly created in monasteries, but she knew that commercial scriptoria eventually appeared in big cities, like Paris. What one was doing buried in the south of France was anybody's guess.

A mystery.

She loved mysteries.

Her friend Nicodème, who curated the Museum of Mysteries in Eze, loved them too and might be of some assistance. Perhaps she'd give him a call.

Right now, she needed to protect the find.

She lifted the book, set it back inside the chest, and turned to leave.

A chill ran down her spine. Where'd that come from? She glanced around at the construction site.

Nothing unusual or strange in sight.

So she walked away.

Bothered.

Chapter 2

CASSIOPEIA POURED HER MORNING CUP OF BLACK COFFEE AND SAT AT the rector's table with her toast and two hard boiled eggs. Aristotle said *all human actions have one or more of seven causes. Chance, nature, compulsions, habit, reason, passion, desire.* For her, habit seemed most prevalent, though the *passion* part sounded better every day.

She wondered what Cotton was doing.

They'd not been able to see one another for nearly two weeks.

He was the love of her life. That much she now knew. But where their relationship was headed seemed unknown. They stayed apart more than together and she often wondered if that was what fueled their desire. Both of them were type-A personalities who liked their space. But they cherished each other too. They'd made a pact not to lie to one another and to always be honest about their feelings. But they'd both violated that agreement on more than one occasion. Still, he was her best friend and she his, and that said it all.

She opened her laptop and perused online copies of *L'Indépendent, Midi Libre,* and *La Tribune.* Not much happening in the world today. When she clicked on the daily edition of *Nouvelles de l'art* she saw that the art news periodical featured a familiar photograph.

The gold casket from yesterday.

She navigated to an interior page with an article and more images, all taken, as noted, *at the medieval construction site of Givors.* There was a shot of the Book of Hours' cover with its rose window decoration. A close-up of the historiated letter O with its illustration of the Annunciation to the

Virgin. And another of the book opened to a double page, spread out in all its glory. Wrapped around the photos was text describing the discovery, all with Shelby Randall's photo credit and byline.

She shook her head.

Shelby should have asked if it was all right to publish the pictures and the story. They'd had an agreement that nothing would be released without prior approval. Granted, publicity for the dig site was always welcome. That was why she'd allowed the woman to be there in the first place. Donations in the hundreds of thousands of euros came in each year from public and charitable foundations, all going toward the building costs, which she supplemented with her personal fortune. School groups and college interns were a regular. Every summer she held a two-week symposium, open to credentialed historians.

But this was exploitation.

And Shelby had ignored their agreement.

That matter needed immediate attention.

She stood and left the dining room, heading back upstairs to her bedroom on the second floor to change into work clothes. The chateau was four storied, and there was nothing feudal about it, as it had been built with comfort and beauty as a nobleman's hunting lodge. By the time she bought it, the building was deteriorating. She'd restored the original look outside and gutted the inside, keeping the feel, but installing all of the modern conveniences. None of the former bareness existed, nor was it over-luxuriant with irrelevant things there to impress people. She'd stuck to period furnishings, though. Which she liked. All here was tranquil and respectable. Her home. So its new name had been symbolic of the peace it provided.

Matval.

Meditative.

She entered her bedroom and heard the doorbell chime. A recording of the ancient ringing in St. Mark's Campanile that she'd had specially recorded.

A visitor?

This early?

She stepped back to the open doorway of her bedroom and heard the voice of her major domo, Bernard, who'd been caretaker of the chateau since she bought it. Cotton Malone sat at the top of the list of those she trusted implicitly. Bernard was a close second. She heard the door close, then footsteps climbing to the second floor. She retreated into her bathroom, waiting for Bernard's soft knock, which came.

She invited him in.

"A gentleman to see you," he said. "*Monsieur* Roland Beláncourt." Bernard handed her a card. "No appointment. And quite early in the day."

She caught the reservation in his voice that said, *yet the man had driven all the way out here to see her.*

She studied the card and noticed the discreet logo of a blue wing with gold trim in the upper right corner. The Beláncourt name and that logo was plastered on the sides of planes all over the world. It was an aerospace giant that built jets, missiles, stealth fighters, even spacecraft for the European Space Research people. She'd seen Roland Beláncourt's picture in newspapers and magazines and remembered the story of how, as a boy, he'd almost been killed after the small plane he and his father were flying crashed. Rather than avoid the sky, the incident spurred him on to become an aerospace engineer, making billions in the process.

He was also a generous philanthropist. Especially to Catholic causes. She recalled reading an article about a tiny chapel near Cannes where he'd paid to renovate an altar painting that turned out to be an original Tintoretto. He then hired an artist to create a copy for the chapel and arranged for the original to hang in the Louvre.

Now he was here.

Unannounced.

Before eight in the morning.

And she was curious.

She entered the library.

The room was lined with bookshelves from floor to ceiling, two stories high. Over eight thousand volumes. Most quite valuable. Some from her grandfather and father's collection she'd inherited, most she'd bought herself. Cotton, as a lifelong bibliophile, loved her collection. A spiral staircase tucked into one corner wound up to a railed gallery that cat-walked around the room and offered access to the upper shelves. She'd always liked the view from up there.

Beláncourt appeared utterly at ease as he greeted her.

He was tall, tawny of hair and moustache, and broad shouldered. His face was clean shaven, highlighting dark, wary eyes and a sly curve to thin lips. He wore an expensive suit, tailor cut to his slim frame, and fashionable Italian loafers. The clear aristocratic stature, his lean aquiline jawline, and the fine prominence of his cheekbones all screamed of a man who stayed in perfect command over himself.

But this was her home.

Where she was in charge.

"So good to meet you," she said in French. "To what do I owe the pleasure of this unannounced visit at so early an hour?"

"Your castle project is quite impressive. I took a moment and admired it before knocking on your door."

She caught the misdirection. He was posturing. Trying to assume control.

"How can I help you?" she asked, not offering him a seat.

"No coffee or tea?"

"I'm assuming you've already had your breakfast. I have a full schedule today. And, as I mentioned, we don't have an appointment. So how can I help you?"

"I apologize for being so bold. But I can be impatient when I want something."

"And what is it you want?"

"I would like to purchase the illustrated manuscript you recently discovered. Simply name your price."

News traveled fast. "You saw the article in *Nouvelles de l'art?*"

"I did."

"And came straight here?"

He smiled. "The advantages of owning a fast helicopter."

"It's not for sale."

"I'm willing to pay *any* price you ask. Think of how much faster your construction project would go with a heavy infusion of cash."

"I'm not poor. Which I'm sure you already know."

"Of course. Terra is well known around the world. I am quite familiar with your family's company."

She ignored the compliment, which seemed designed to disarm her.

"The manuscript isn't for sale. At any price. It's going to be part of the exhibition of rare medieval objects found here at the site when our museum eventually opens."

"How admirable. But I would like to add your find to my own

collection."

"Unfortunately, that's not possible."

"You do understand the meaning of *any* price?" he asked.

"Do you understand the meaning of the word no?"

"*Mademoiselle* Vitt, this will all be much more amicable if you just name a price and we make a deal."

She almost smiled at his persistence. "I don't imagine this is going to be amicable at all. There simply is no price."

He sighed. "I was hoping that we would be able to come to terms. There is always a price. Today it was to be money. Tomorrow?" He shrugged. "Who knows?"

She caught the hint of a threat.

"Let it not be said that I did not try." He gave her a slight bow before turning for the door. "No need to show me out. I can find the way. And, *Mademoiselle* Vitt, please know that my initial offer is always my best offer. From that point on, my negotiations only go down."

He walked toward the door.

"*Monsieur* Beláncourt."

He stopped and faced her.

"If you ever come here again. Which I hope you don't. Call first."

Chapter 3

THE *PERFECTI* LEANED AGAINST THE ROUGH TRUNK OF A TALL PINE AND used its low-hanging branches and spring needles as camouflage. Sunlight sieved through the canopy overhead, spotting the ground. The sodden forest around her reeked with the dank smell of soaked earth.

Cassiopeia Vitt's chateau stood in the distance in a sheltered hollow, trees all around affording maximum seclusion. Its four levels of dark red stone and brick were arranged in artistically symmetrical patterns, topped by a slate roof and framed by ivy-crowned towers. The old moat remained, a mere remnant of its former glory, now filled with emerald grass.

And thus, they say, God created His angels of such nature from the beginning that they could at their pleasure do good or evil, and they call this 'free will' or, according to some of them, 'choice.' Both mean a certain free strength, or power, by which he to whom it is given is equally capable of good or evil.

She muttered the ancient words from the Book of Two Principles, which always seemed to bring strength in times of stress.

Like now.

Such a peaceful picture the chateau offered. She knew its name. *Matval.* Peace. It seemed fitting. And if she cared about aesthetics she might be impressed by the wealth and stature the building represented, along with the remarkable castle that was being erected not far away, but she'd never been swayed by the accoutrements of refinement. Money meant nothing, power even less. What she cared about was a resurrection. A redemption of the *Bons Òmes,* Good Men, *Bonas Femnas,*

Good Women, and *Bons Crestians*, the Good Christians.

She watched through her binoculars as Roland Beláncourt emerged from the chateau's front door. She'd been shocked to see him drive up a few minutes ago. He'd apparently noticed the archeological find online too and moved fast. But he was leaving empty handed. That meant he'd not been able to buy the book.

May he rot on this earth for eternity.

He had no right to the sacred object. None at all. If the book pictured in the online article was what she believed it to be, then it belonged to the faithful.

And no one else.

A Google alert she'd maintained for years had sent her to the *Nouvelles de l'art* site. Of the posted images, two had offered critical clues. The first had been the book's cover detailing the rose window and cross. The second was the photo of two facing inside pages, rich with illustration, the text all in Occitan. In the highly decorative artwork she'd noticed the Cathar symbols. She'd also spotted the repeated Occitan crosses creating a patterned background on the right side of the page. Interwoven into the crosses were stylized doves. That bird could be found carved in the same sleek way into rocks throughout the Languedoc, where Cathars once flourished in abundance. A free flying dove symbolized peace, of being in a state of grace, of being held close in God's wonderful love.

Come ye blessed of my Father, possess you the kingdom prepared for you from the foundation of the world. For I was hungry and you gave me to eat. I was thirsty and you gave me to drink.

She was sure.

The map had been found.

And now she stood a few hundred meters away from that precious book. Elated on the one hand, relieved on the other that Beláncourt had walked out without it, but frustrated that she had no idea how to obtain it.

She'd traveled to Givors to meet the woman she'd read about in the story. Cassiopeia Vitt. Definitely a person of power and wealth. But also of the past. A lover of history. Which might bode well. Perhaps Vitt would at least show her the book. Just a few moments with it might be enough to learn its secret. Beláncourt showing up here seemed an unexpected verification that this could be it. He owned one of the largest collections of illuminated manuscripts in private hands. But he'd left the chateau without it. Which meant she had no chance to buy it either, especially since her financial resources were infinitesimal compared to an aerospace magnate.

Bless us, bless us, O Lord God, the Father of the spirits of good men, and help us in all that we wish to do.

And help was what she needed.

The ancient souls protecting the book had made sure she'd come here. The good spirits that guided all her waking actions had determined that she would reach this spot just behind Beláncourt.

Why?

That was obvious.

So she would know her enemy.

Piss on the Catholics.

Eight hundred years had passed since the pope declared war on the Cathars, all backed by a hollow promise. *Give us forty days' service and your place in Paradise will be assured. All your sins will be forgiven, and not only those you have committed, but also any that you may now commit.*

What a lie.

That war had been something new. Not a fight against infidels. Instead, a campaign of Christians killing Christians.

The Albigensian Crusade.

And for nearly fifty years the people of the Languedoc had been systematically slaughtered.

The main target?

Bons Crestians.

Who'd grown in numbers and influence. A new form of Christianity that stretched across what would later be called northern Spain and southern France, known then as Occitània.

A place of unique cultural identity. Where the races blended to produce strong, determined individuals who respected truth and character. Much more aligned with Aragon and Catalonia than Paris, there were different forms of land ownership, different ways to inherit, even another language, *Occitan.*

Which had all added up to a threat.

The word Cathar evolved from the Greek *katharos*, meaning pure. And a simple mandate governed. No one who did not live the teachings of Christ could minister to others. Title meant nothing. Money even less. Only the intrinsic value of the soul counted. No matter a person's standing in life, noble or the poorest of peasant, the same opportunity to preach was available to all.

Man or woman.

For the Cathars they were equal.

Cathars had no need for a church to intercede with God on their behalf. Instead, Christ was directly accessible. They believed that the earthly world, all the majesty of nature that now surrounded her, was the work of the God of Evil, created as a distraction. The God of Good, the Pure Spirit, was incapable of creating physical matter. The inhabitants of the earth were but spirits, trapped here in physical bodies, in a place of the devil's creation, until such time as they could transform and ascend to the God of Good.

There were two types of believers.

Simple, who were the vast majority.

And the perfected ones.

The *Perfecti*.

Good Men and Women who vowed to live an ideal life, in service, ministering to the believers. They swore to take no life of any creature having breath, whether human or animal, and eat no meat. They refrained from carnal activities, from lying, taking oaths, or speaking ill of others. They held close the faith of Christ and his gospel, as the apostles taught, not how a church redefined them. So devoted were they that, among the thousands tortured and killed by the Albigensian crusaders, only one *Perfecti* ever betrayed the faith.

Piss on his soul.

The Good Ones also despised the Cross. A crucified Christ was an impossibility. Jesus was created by God, a physical man not to be crucified, but a spirit to lead others toward a better existence. They worshipped Christ, the Son of Mary, but not in the same way as Catholics. Incense, oils, statues, churches, and sacraments were all creations of the physical world, inherently evil distractions, which must be avoided.

It all made sense.

And people believed by the thousands.

They abandoned the appalling simony of the Catholic clergy, who extorted tithes, kept mistresses, and sold sacraments. The extreme purity of life and disinterest in wealth won the Cathars respect from the local nobility. Even better the Good Ones represented no threat to temporal power, unlike Rome who continually meddled in politics. The simplicity of dualism outweighed the pope's heavy hand. And when the Bishop of Toulouse openly censured the Catholic clergy and denounced the Church, things began to come to a head.

Priests were sent to sway the faithful back into the fold.

When that failed, armies came next, doing *God's business*, calling themselves *pilgrims*.

Piss on them too.

So many sieges.

Béziers, Carcassonne, Bram, Lavaur, Lastours, Saissac, Minerve, Termes, Les Cassés, Puivert, Toulouse, Muret, Castelnaudary, Foix, Beaucaire, Marmande.

So many burnings. Torture. Death.

Her heart still hurt for the suffering.

Unlike their fellow Christians, Cathars were pacifists and did not fight back. Instead, the local nobles took up arms for them, trying to repel the invaders. It all ended in 1244 with the fall of Montségur, though Cathars continued to be burned alive for another hundred years.

Piss on the Inquisition.

Although He knew fully and foresaw from eternity the fate of all His angels, His wisdom and providence did not make His angels become demons. They became demons and things of evil by their own will, because they did not wish to remain holy and humble before their Lord, but wickedly puffed themselves up in pride against Him.

The time had come for a rebirth.

The Good Men and Women would live again.

But to accomplish that she needed the Book of Hours. Standing in the woods adjacent to Cassiopeia Vitt's chateau, she now knew that the God of Good had bestowed a second chance.

The message clear.

Come what may. No matter what it took. She must prevail.

She heard a noise behind her and turned.

A deer emerged from the woods, then meandered off.

She smiled at the wonder.

Death did not scare her. It never scared a Cathar. For it was merely a release from this evil world. A moment of freedom, when the soul would finally ascend to the God of Good's realm, leaving the devil behind.

That lack of fear gave her an edge.

One she planned to use to full advantage.

Chapter 4

Cassiopeia glanced at the clock.

7:28 a.m.

Yesterday had been a mixed bag. First the unexpected visit of Roland Beláncourt, then the rest of the day spent mulling over the significance of a book from some eight hundred years ago. Last night sleep had been hard to find and, when it finally arrived, it came in fitful bursts. Beláncourt's parting comment kept echoing through her mind. *Please know that my initial offer is always my best offer. From that point on, my negotiations only go down.*

Definitely a warning.

Luckily, it took a lot more than that to scare her.

In her bathrobe, she stood in the kitchen and waited at the espresso machine as it delivered its magical elixir into a tiny Limoges cup. During her remodeling the original 17th century kitchen had been removed and the room restored to somewhat of its original appearance from three hundred years ago, save for the addition of modern appliances, most sheathed with veneers that matched the wainscoting on the walls. Clever and imaginative. But also functional. The interior designer she'd employed from Marseille had done an excellent job.

Her parents had instilled in her a sense of purpose, responsibility, and independence. From that came confidence. Her training in martial arts and in the use of firearms had further boosted her self-esteem.

Yes, she knew fear.

But she also knew how to control it.

She carried her espresso from the kitchen and navigated a labyrinthine set of hallways to her private study. The cozy space had originally been a smoking room that the Duc of Givors had utilized after building the first chateau. Dark dreary rooms, no matter how well lit, depressed her. So she'd stripped the walls and replaced the paneling with a light, airy plaster, keeping the rich moldings and intricate parquet floor. Two walls were fronted by bookshelves that, unlike the library where it was all collectibles, were her personal books, on subjects like architecture, history and mythology. Her Roentgen writing desk faced the east wall, where French doors led out to a stone terrace edging a rose garden.

She opened the doors and allowed in the morning breeze. Clumps of laurel and honeysuckle bloomed. As did the roses. While breeding roses to be infection-resistant, scientists had sacrificed smell for hardiness. She'd searched out the older breeds like Cécile Brünner, Marie Pavié, and the Fairy, which retained their intoxicating waft. True, they were much more work and a bit fragile, but worth it.

Like so much in life.

She sat at her desk, opened the laptop, and switched on the music. Her morning fare consisted of Gregorian chants, and the sonorous otherworldly tones of the Benedictine Monks filled the room. She loved the sounds, which reached deep into her soul and soothed her psyche. The power of music healed. No question. She'd seen that happen with animals, children, the sick, and the elderly. There was something unexplained about its unfelt power. Not God. Not magic. Just a tonic for the soul.

She sipped her coffee and enjoyed the moment.

She loved her parents for leaving her a life of such freedom and choice. Had she been the best daughter? Hard to say. But they'd been wonderful parents.

She laid the cup down and clicked on the email icon, perusing the list to see what, if anything, required immediate attention. Those from *Terra* corporate headquarters would have to be read. But later. As the sole shareholder and owner, she was kept informed of major decisions. Not micro-management, as that was not her style, but enough for her to be informed.

She forwarded three emails with subject interview request to the publicist she kept on retainer, the same one who'd recommended Shelby. Like Cotton would say, she and Shelby *would have to take a trip to the woodshed.* Nothing the young woman had done had been good. She saw a response to a note, with images, she'd sent the day before to an illuminated manuscript scholar at Paris' Collège de France asking for help with her find. The professor expressed an interest in working with her.

The laptop dinged.

A new e-mail.

From Cotton.

She clicked off the music, opened it, and saw only a link. She shook her head and smiled. A romantic he was not. And while he rarely spoke of matters of the heart, she never doubted how he felt about her.

She clicked on the link, which sent her to a video about a Russian oligarch who they'd dealt with a few years ago. The oligarch's wife had supposedly committed suicide, but the Russian internal police had arrested the oligarch for murder. Unusual, to say the least. Money bought power in Russia. But, apparently, their former nemesis had fallen out of favor. She agreed with the short note Cotton had typed above the link. Couldn't happen to a nicer guy.

A shout arose outside.

She sprang from the chair and rushed out the open French doors. On the lawn, just beyond the rose garden, Viktor and Shelby chased a hooded figure, yelling for the person to stop.

What was going on?

The figure was fast, with a solid head start, disappearing into the trees just as Shelby fell hard to the ground. Viktor kept going, but Cassiopeia rushed to see if Shelby was all right. Joining the pursuit seemed impractical in a bathrobe, considering she had little on underneath.

"Are you hurt?" she asked.

"The...book," Shelby said, panting hard. "Get...the book."

"Someone has the manuscript?"

Shelby nodded, fighting to catch her breath. "I'm...okay. The bitch whacked me...in the head with a...metal tray. My head is...spinning. Get...the book."

"No need," Viktor said as he ran up.

His face was scratched and there was a thin stream of blood trickling down his right cheek. He was holding the plastic container with the Book of Hours.

"I got it. Hopefully unharmed."

He handed it to her.

"Which is more than I can say for your face," Cassiopeia said.

He waved away the injury. "I ran through the orchard. I managed to tackle whoever it was, but she kicked me in the gut and got away." He pointed. "She left that behind."

This was a first. A full-fledged theft attempt. Dogs patrolled the construction site at night, there to chase off deer and boar who made a mess of things. But they'd never employed anything grander.

"We're too lax around here about security," Viktor said. "Maybe it's time to institute some new protocols."

Maybe so. "But I don't want to start living like I'm in a prison."

Still—

That made two people interested in the manuscript.

Or, maybe only one, making two different attempts.

From that point on, my negotiations only go down.

Time for her to pay Roland Beláncourt a visit.

Chapter 5

THE *PERFECTI'S* LEG ACHED.

Her escape from Cassiopeia Vitt's chateau had aggravated an old injury. But what hurt more was that the God of Evil had prevailed.

It behooves us of necessity to confess that there is another principle, one of evil, who works most wickedly against the true God and His creation, and this principle seems to move God against His own creation and the creation against its God.

The God of Good wanted her to have the manuscript. Why else had she been sent here? That certainty had become even clearer when she found no obstacles to walking right across the grounds without anyone noticing. She'd watched yesterday as Cassiopeia Vitt had taken the Book of Hours from the chateau to an out-building labeled *Laboratoire.* When Vitt departed empty-handed she'd known the prize had been left inside. She'd wanted to make her retrieval last night, but the worksite was patrolled by dogs who kept a steady watch, never abandoning their post. The animals had not been taken away until a little after seven a.m.

That's when she made her move.

Only a handful of people had been around, so she'd hustled across the site, using the various waste piles and work sheds for cover, her head sheathed in a black hood. At the lab she'd forced the door open, which was restricted only by a simple door lock. Inside, she'd found the book, tucked safe inside a plastic bin. She'd opened the container, seen the worn leather cover and rose window, then caressed the exterior with her fingertips, feeling the glory that God washed through her. She'd replaced the lid and was preparing to leave when the devil interfered.

"What are you doing?" a female voice asked.

She'd whirled to see a woman at the lab's door, who advanced her way.

Take unto you the armor of God that you may be able to resist in the evil day, and to stand in all things perfect, wherewith you may be able to extinguish all the fiery darts of the most wicked one.

The threat had to be dealt with.

She'd grabbed a stainless steel tray and slammed it into the woman's head, stunning, but not disabling her. The woman lunged. They both went down and she brought a knee into her attacker's stomach. Which allowed her to roll to her feet, grab the plastic bin, and rush from the lab. She'd abandoned caution and raced across the open grass, past the chateau, toward the trees. Someone yelled stop. A quick glance back and she saw the woman from the lab and a man about fifty meters behind. But racing her way. The woman had fallen in her pursuit, but the man kept coming.

Her throat had burned from heavy breathing, her knees ached.

But she'd kept running.

Then something slammed into her from behind. Her legs folded beneath her, head snapped back, air squirted from her lungs as she hit the ground hard, two arms wrapped around her waist. The grip relaxed and she used that instant to wrench herself free and kick the man in the chest. He rolled to one side, the breath leaving him, and she sprang to her feet.

He ignored her and grabbed the plastic bin.

Could she take him?

Probably not.

So she'd fled, finding her car and driving away.

How awful.

She'd searched for so long, the better part of the past decade devoted to the quest, one clue leading the way. Not in the preferred Occitan. But in French.

Le livre de roses conduira au lac de l'apprentissage mènerae.

The rose book will lead to the Lake of Learning.

She'd studied every existing treatise and text, which weren't many. Examined every carving, sculpture, and artifact that was, in any way, tied to Cathar history. She'd long lived in southern France. Breathed air that contained particles of the same dust that her ancestors had inhaled. She might well have been one of them centuries ago, her soul reborn over and over into envelopes of sinful flesh. Going through cycles of life, searching, wanting, seeking a final release.

She had to find the Lake of Learning.

Yet she'd failed.

Again.

Tears formed in her eyes.

What to do next? More important, what would Vitt do next? Everything she'd read suggested Cassiopeia Vitt was highly intelligent and rational. A collector, but not a fanatic. An historian and architect. Clearly a risk taker. The fact that someone had tried to steal the book would not be taken lightly. Would she blame Beláncourt? Possibly. No, probably. So maybe the way to possess the Book of Hours was to take it after Beláncourt managed to obtain it?

Allowing him do the heavy lifting first.

Her car kept heading for Toulouse and she turned over the options in her mind. Vitt would go to Beláncourt and confront the man whom she believed had attempted the robbery. When? Today? Tomorrow?

Hard to say.

But she would go.

The drive west took five hours, which included one stop for the bathroom, some hot coffee, and an apple. The pain in her knee continued to throb. She drove straight to Beláncourt Aerospace and parked in the visitor's lot, her car blending with the hundreds already there. The facility's main entrance sat across the street and she told herself to be mindful of the cameras that surely watched every square centimeter.

What was the saying?

Keep your friends close and your enemies closer.

Roland Beláncourt, the papist, was perhaps her greatest enemy. She knew his habits and haunts. His likes and dislikes. His wants and desires. The time was approaching 1:30 p.m., so he was just finishing lunch. He liked to take his midday meal at Emile's on Saint-Georges Square, later than most people. Right on cue, at 1:45 his chauffeured Rolls Royce motored through the gate without stopping for the guard. Later, he would leave the office at 6 p.m. Dinner was always at home, in his chateau that sat a few kilometers out of town. The only exception came if he had a meeting or an event, which was rare, as he liked to end his work day early. He was in bed by nine and up at five a.m. Nothing mattered now but the book and the possibility that, after so many centuries, its secrets may finally be within reach. Her first attempt had been dismal. She could not fail this time.

At 2:20 p.m. her vigilance was rewarded.

A car approached the main gate and she saw the driver.

Cassiopeia Vitt.

Chapter 6

Cassiopeia drove onto the premises of Beláncourt Aerospace. Her first visit, though she'd seen the massive industrial complex while flying in and out of Toulouse, as it sat adjacent to the main airport.

Her home, Givors, was a beautiful place to live. The ancient city sat on the confluence of the Rivers Rhone and Gier. Wooded fields and mountains rose all around, especially to the south where her chateau and castle project were located. The city was originally known for its coal and pottery industries, but both had long died away. Now it was mostly a bedroom community for those who worked in nearby Lyon, approximately a half hour drive away.

Which was the closest airport.

But she'd not had the time to drive to Lyon and wait for the next commuter flight, so she'd arranged for a direct helicopter trip from her chateau to Toulouse. Her father had taught her that some indulgences were worth the price, especially when they saved time, which was one commodity that money could not buy. When he died, far too young at age seventy-two, he'd more than proved his point. Her mother passed a few months later, some say from a broken heart. Occasionally she engaged in wishful thinking that they were still alive, back at home in Spain. An impossibility, she knew, but the dream soothed the raw edges of grief that still rose.

During the flight, she'd read up on Roland Beláncourt.

Born and raised in Toulouse, he'd attended university nearby and, after graduating, started Beláncourt Aeronautics, a small company that manufactured recreational aircraft. Now the conglomerate, known as Beláncourt Aerospace, employed over ten thousand people and, along with Airbus, Air France Industries, and Dassault Aviation, it had become one of the top five corporations in Aerospace Valley—the land between Toulouse and Bordeaux—so called because there were more than five hundred aviation companies clustered in the region.

Personal information about Beláncourt, though, seemed more sketchy.

He was a well-known philanthropist, creating endowments at the Aeronautics, Space and Civil Aviation departments at his alma mater, the Université Fédérale de Toulouse Midi-Pyrénées, one of the oldest in France. Established in 1229, if she wasn't mistaken. Perhaps about the time when the Book of Hours had been created. In addition to scholarly donations, Beláncourt also gave generously to historic renovation, especially religious buildings. She'd also read an account of his rebuilding of the cloister and ramparts of the Cathédrale Saint-Étienne de Toulouse, whose unusual architecture was renowned within the region.

Like her father, Beláncourt was an avid art collector, which he lent out to museums around the world. Little about his family situation existed other than he'd once been married, but that union had ended, after eleven years, with no children. There were women in his life, the most recent a well-respected novelist, Nina St. Clair, whose books Cassiopeia enjoyed, but nothing to suggest he was a playboy.

She stepped from the car and faced a glass building with the corporate logo emblazoned in cobalt above the entrance. Arranging the meeting had been simple. A call to Beláncourt telling him she wanted to discuss the book and a car had been waiting for her at the nearby heliport when she landed.

Inside, she was greeted by a placid blonde woman with a capable air and a kindly face, who led her back outside through a rear door, toward a row of hangars. On the way she was asked if she'd like any refreshments. Water sounded good, so she put in a request. Their destination was one of the smaller hangars adorned with the blue logo and she was surprised to see the entire inside comprised Beláncourt's executive office.

The entrance was divided into three separate spaces. Most likely for assistants. A set of oak doors led into a cavernous room with walls of caramel colored leather affixed with rivets, the arched ceiling identical to the silver sheet metal exterior. That color combination echoed in the modernistic design woven into a massive floor rug. Couches and chairs were covered in the same caramel leather. Beláncourt's desk, and a long conference table with chairs around it, were fashioned from what looked like airplane wings. A few choice paintings and lithographs adorned the walls.

Then there were the artifacts.

On a table against the wall stood a Tibetan buddha. Several other busts rested atop pedestals. Shelves displayed old volumes of biology and nature, well bound in cloth casings. One cabinet with glass-fronted drawers held oracle bones and what appeared to be megalodon teeth. A stereoscope displayed a collection of centuries- old views. It all had the feel of a museum, untouched by human warmth.

"I couldn't be happier to see you," Beláncourt said, staying with French, standing from his desk and walking toward her.

He was dressed, as yesterday, unwrinkled, in a dark suit, stiff-collared shirt, and silk tie. His face was smoothly shaved, his hair brushed into place, the brown eyes clear and steady. The woman who'd escorted her poured a glass of Evian and squeezed a slice of lime into it. She accepted the glass and enjoyed a few sips. "I'm not sure you'll be so happy to see me after you've heard what I have to say."

He looked perplexed. "I'm a grown man. I can handle it."

"Your attempt to steal the book this morning failed."

His expression changed from one of bewilderment to concern. "I'm disturbed to hear that something like that happened. Truly, I am. But, I assure you, *my* attempts never fail."

"And yet you've failed twice with me."

He chuckled. "I like you. You're direct, and that is refreshing."

"I'm sorry, but I can't say the same about you."

"I assure you, I made no attempt to steal that book. None at all."

"And why don't I believe you?"

"Because I'm suspect in your eyes. And I understand how you would think I might try such a thing. But, again, it was not me."

For all the distaste she held for Beláncourt, something troubled her. Either he was a world-class liar, which was possible, or he really didn't know what she was talking about.

"I assume you're not here, then, to sell me the manuscript," he said.

She enjoyed more of the water and decided a little misdirection on her part would be good. "You went to a lot of trouble creating this office.

Quite an effort."

"I don't care for ordinary. I prefer things to be different."

"This space certainly qualifies."

She liked strong men. But where Cotton tempered his strength with humility and compassion, Beláncourt oozed pride and arrogance. And that she detested. But she detected no lies, no embellishing flourishes to provide a stronger feeling of truth. No warning flags. "Someone tried to steal the manuscript this morning. A woman, we believe. Her head was hooded. She managed to escape, but we were able to save the book."

"That's good to hear. But I don't steal things. I buy them. That book is worth, at most, a hundred thousand euros. I'd gladly pay twice that right now."

"You were quite emphatic yesterday that your next offer would be much different," she said. "You were right. It is different. Now you're offering double its value?"

"You have no idea what my offer yesterday would have been. We never got that far in our discussion."

Good point. "Surely you can see how I would assume that you were behind the theft, trying to obtain the book for nothing."

He nodded. "But it was not me."

Which begged the question. "Then who?"

He shrugged. "Could be an art thief, after something to sell. There are many who make their living peddling stolen objects. The person probably saw the same internet postings we all did and thought it an easy thing to acquire, considering the remoteness of your property."

That was entirely plausible. Still. "Why is the book so important to you?"

"I collect objects of knowledge and beauty. Books of Hours are of a particular interest. I saw the images online and they spoke to me. I had to have it."

Now she felt he was lying. This was not about art. Or a collector's lust. Something else was at play here.

"I have one of the largest private collections of illuminated manuscripts in the world," he said. "I would love to show them to you."

Now he was trying charm.

"*Monsieur* Beláncourt, I don't believe in coincidences. I'm still not totally convinced you were not behind the theft attempt today. But I will take you at your word. I came to tell you again, to your face, that the manuscript is not for sale. Please stop your efforts to obtain it." She paused. "Whatever they might be."

"I'm afraid that is quite impossible."

Now she was puzzled. "Why?"

He stood at attention, hands folded behind his back. "As I mentioned, I would never steal anything. But my statement to you yesterday still holds. My next offer will not be anything close to two hundred thousand euros."

There was that arrogance again.

"As you will soon learn," he said, "the ways I go about obtaining what I want are much more effective than robbery."

She did not like the sound of that.

His lean face creased into an irritating smile.

"*Au revoir, mademoiselle.*"

Chapter 7

CASSIOPEIA GREETED THE CHAIRMAN OF THE BOARD, JEAN PAUL WEIL, and the company's legal counsel, Marie L'Etoile. Both had worked for her father, and now worked for her at *Terra*. Two days had passed since her meeting with Roland Beláncourt in Toulouse, his last words a clear threat that he'd seemed unfazed with issuing.

Jean Paul and Marie had flown the four hundred kilometers south from Paris to meet with her. In her father's day the corporation had been headquartered in Barcelona. But she'd relocated after some unfavorable changes to Spanish tax laws. The French had been far more accommodating in offering an incentive package for a multi-billion euro corporate headquarters that employed over five hundred people. So she'd moved the company to France and changed its name to *Terra*. Earth. Her father would have surely approved, since he was the first to say what Virgil believed. *Fortune sides with him who dares.* Or, in this case, *she who dares.*

She led them into a comfortable den that had once been the chateau's music room. The original gilded molding, consisting of violins, horns, and flutes scattered amongst garlands of flowers, drew the eye. It stood in contrast to the walls and ceiling, a shade of celadon green usually found in a cat's eye. An oversize celadon carpet protected the centuries-old parquet floor. A tray of coffee and biscuits waited on a table. She served her guests, then inquired about their visit.

"We have a matter of concern," Jean Paul said. "We've never seen anything like this before, so we thought it best to come in person."

Nothing about that sounded good.

"Over the last forty-eight hours we've lost six major contracts that were under negotiation," he said. "We've also been told that we are ineligible for a dozen more contracts here in France, Belgium, Holland, and Italy due to litigation that has been started against us."

Cassiopeia looked over at Marie. "What are we being sued for?"

"Late deliveries, substandard materials, overcharging. Two even allege fraud."

She was shocked. Never had the company faced such accusations.

"We came to assure you," Jean Paul said, "before these matters become public, that we have not engaged in any of those irregularities."

"All of the suits are frivolous," Marie added. "I can deal with them, but it will take time and money to clear each off the court dockets. There will also be a public relations effect to our reputation. We could have some irreversible losses in the hundreds of millions of euros."

"Tell me more," she said.

Jean Paul opened his Louis Vuitton briefcase, removed a laptop, and found a spreadsheet. She leaned in, looked over his shoulder, and studied the information.

"The contracts at issue all deal with platinum and silver, two of the most popular metals we sell. Not overly large quantities, but expensive and highly profitable."

"Let me guess," she said. "All of these involve aviation?"

"That's correct," Marie said. "We are one of the major suppliers of precious metals to that industry, and have been for a long time. That's why these cancellations are so surprising. They are from long-time customers."

"Are any a subsidiary of Beláncourt Aeronautical?"

Marie scanned the list. "At least half."

No surprise.

As you will soon learn, the ways I go about obtaining what I want are much more effective than robbery.

The guy had balls, she'd give him that.

"You look like you know what this is about," Jean Paul said.

"Fortunately, I do."

She spoke with Jean Paul and Marie for another hour, devising a strategy to defend against the onslaught. The lawsuits spanned three different jurisdictions across Europe, but *Terra's* legal department was up to the challenge. She told them to answer the allegations, deny them all, and leave the rest to her. She explained nothing about Beláncourt's threat, only that she knew the source of the problem and would be in touch. After they left she headed for her study, where the Book of Hours was locked away in a wall safe.

She retrieved the plastic bin and sat at her desk.

What made this volume so special?

Books of Hours were first created by monks for use by fellow monks, detailing the appropriate prayers for specific hours of the day, weeks, months, and seasons. She knew they always began with a liturgical calendar, a list of feast days in chronological order, which was also a way of calculating the date of Easter.

But this one had no such calendar.

Normally, each section of the prayers was also accompanied by an illustration to help the reader meditate on the subject. Biblical scenes, saints, slices from rural life, or displays of royal splendor were common. The illustrations were called miniatures, and not because the images were small. Instead, *miniature* had its origins in the Latin *miniare,* meaning "to illuminate."

This one had few such images.

Instead symbols dominated.

An odd configuration of lines and circles.

Latin was also the preferred language. Yet this one was in Occitan, the language of the Languedoc, once favored by the troubadours. Eight hundred years ago most people in southern France would have spoken it. Today, it was far more parochial, but it had survived. Occasionally, some street signs or placards would appear in both French and Occitan. But, overall, it was not something heard in widespread use, more a form of communication used at home, between friends and family. She'd learned to speak it while at university, and it was regularly utilized by the workers at the construction site. Almost no manuscripts written in it from ancient times had survived.

Except this one.

Books of Hours were generally created on parchment or vellum, specially treated to receive the pigment. She also knew about the ink. Iron gall, made from the gallnuts on oak trees, where wasp larvae were laid, tinted through the use of various minerals. The writing was generally done with a feathered quill pen. The most vivid and expensive dye was *lapis lazuli*, a blue gemstone with gold flecks which, during the Middle Ages, was found only in present-day Afghanistan.

This tome seemed heavy with that blue.

Rare, but not unusual.

This book's creators had used plenty of gold and silver leaf to marvelous effect, providing even more *illumination* to the pages.

Her radar screamed at full alert. Roland Belâncourt had gone to a lot of trouble to gain her undivided attention.

Just to acquire a book for his collection?

No way.

She reached for her cell phone and dialed the number on the card Belâncourt had left. An assistant connected her straight to him and she could almost see the smug smile on his face. No sense bothering with amenities. "All right. You have my attention."

"I thought my message would be clear. Perhaps now we can have a more balanced conversation."

"How far are you going to go with this?"

"Whatever is necessary."

"Why is this book so important?"

He did not immediately answer her. Finally, he said, "I could hedge on that answer, or I could just lie to you. But I'm not going to do either. Let us say that the book has a great personal meaning to me. One that I take quite seriously."

That was the second thing he'd said to her that she believed.

"*Monsieur* Belâncourt, you and I have clearly been thrust together. I assume you're not going to leave this be, considering the legal efforts you've already made to force me to this point. I, of course, still do not want to sell. What do you suggest we do now?"

"I have a proposal. Will you allow me to show you something?"

She had no choice. "And what would that be?"

"May I have a half a day of your time tomorrow? If, after that, you no longer wish to sell, then I will allow this matter to drop."

That sounded way too reasonable.

But, again, she had no choice.

"Wear comfortable clothes and boots fit for a climb and hike," he said. "I'll send a plane to pick you up in Lyon at 8 a.m."

Chapter 8

THE *PERFECTI* ENTERED THE HOME AND KNELT. WITH BOTH HANDS folded, she bowed three times saying "Bless me, Lord. Pray for me."

The man who lived there answered her plea. "Lead us to our rightful end."

"God bless you," she told him. "In our prayers, we ask for God to make a good Christian out of us and lead us to our rightful end."

He smiled at her.

She returned his warmth and felt his pain.

The *Melhoramentum* completed, she stood.

She'd driven from Toulouse after watching Beláncourt Aerospace for most of the day. Its owner had come to work, gone to lunch, returned, then left exactly on his regular schedule. Cassiopeia Vitt had not reappeared over the past two days.

A dead end.

And frustrating.

She flushed the anxiety from her mind and tried to concentrate on her duties. Tonight was a special joy, one every *Perfecti* relished in performing. She'd come to this rural farmhouse, near the village of Aug, to perform the *Consolamentum*. Consolation. The laying-on of hands. A spiritual baptism, marking the transition from simple believer to *Perfecti*.

The most sacred ceremony for a Cathar.

No water or submerging was involved, as established by John the Baptist for Catholics. Instead, as practiced by Jesus, this rite depended on the Holy Spirit to penetrate the soul and offer redemption and purity.

Striking in its simplicity, but powerful in effect, the ritual had been handed down from generation to generation of *Bons Crestians*.

"Take me to her," she said.

The old man led her to a small bedchamber. The wan and weak light of a lamp barely lit the room. An elderly woman lay under a colorful quilt. Her face was gaunt, like a cadaver, her thin white hair nearly gone. She'd been sick a long time and death was near. The God of Good was coming to claim another spirit.

She removed the leather-bound gospel from her shoulder bag and held it over the woman's head. "Bless us, bless us, O Lord God, the Father of the spirits of good men, and help us in all that we wish to do."

From the sacred book she removed a sheet of paper upon which she'd printed the Lord's prayer. She handed it to the husband, who slowly read the sacred words aloud.

> *Our father, which art in Heaven,*
> *Hallowed be thy name.*
> *Thy kingdom come,*
> *Thy will be done on Earth as it is in Heaven.*
> *Give us this day our super-substantial bread,*
> *And remit our debts as we forgive our debtors.*
> *And keep us from temptation and free us from evil.*
> *Thine is the kingdom, the power and glory for ever and ever.*

Ordinarily, simple believers would never invoke God in this way, the prayer reserved only for the *Perfecti*. But this was a special occasion. A new soul was being welcomed into the fold, the husband speaking for the wife, who would now become a child of God, with God becoming her father, conferring the right onto her to address Him as *Our Father*.

"Scriptures say that the spirit dwells within the Good Ones, those who have been adopted, as a son, by God," she said. "Tonight I have come to welcome another. Please repeat the Lord's Prayer."

He read the words again.

The old woman lay still, her breathing labored, a slight smile to her thin lips.

"Can she speak?" she asked.

He shook his head. "Not for the last week. I doubt she can hear us either."

"Then you must speak for her."

The *Consolamentum* was usually given to the dying. Simple believers facing imminent death, who were ready to ascend to the next level of faith. Where papists baptized at birth in anticipation of a long life serving the Church, the Good Ones waited until death, when the spirit would finally be free of the evil physical world, headed for the glory of the God of Good. As long as the believer died quickly, no opportunity would come to fall back into sin. But, if the postulant recovered, then he or she became a *Perfecti*, required to live the rest of their life as one.

That did not appear to be a possibility here.

"Do you renounce the harlot church of the persecutors?" she asked the old woman. "Their replica crosses, sham baptisms, and magical rites?" She laid a hand on the woman's shoulder, then touched her head with the Gospel. "I must remind you of all that is forbidden, and all that will be required of you."

The husband bowed his head.

"We are the poor of Christ, who have no fixed abode and flee from city to city like sheep amidst wolves. We are persecuted, as were the apostles and the martyrs, despite the fact that we lead a most strict and holy life, persevering day and night in fasts and abstinence, in prayers, and in labor from which we seek only the necessities. We undergo this because we are not of this world. False apostles, who pollute the word of Christ, who seek after their own interest, will lead you and our fathers astray from the true path. We, and our fathers of apostolic descent, have continued in the grace of God and shall so remain to the end of time. To distinguish us, Christ said *By their fruits you shall know them.* Our fruits consist in following the footsteps of Christ. Pardoning wrongdoers, loving enemies, praying for those who calumniate and accuse, offering the other cheek to the oppressor, giving up one's mantle to him that takes one's tunic, neither judging nor condemning. Will you fulfill these requirements?"

Tears filled the old man's eyes. "She has will and determination. Pray God for her that He give her His strength."

The correct response.

This man had prepared himself well.

"Do you ask pardon for all her past sins?" she asked.

"By the grace of God, I do."

She laid the Gospel upon the old woman's head, her right hand atop the book. Together, she and the husband adored the Father, Son, and Holy Spirit, asking God to welcome His new servant and send down the Holy Spirit to inhabit the postulant's corporal body.

"Repeat after me," she said. "Holy Father, welcome thy servant in thy justice and send upon him thy grace and thy holy spirit."

The old man said the words.

She opened her Gospel to John 1. *"In the beginning was the Word, and the Word was with God, and the Word was God. He was with God in the beginning. Through him all things were made. Without him nothing was made that has been made. In him was life, and that life was the light of all mankind. The light shines in the darkness, and the darkness has not overcome it."*

She smiled down at the old woman. Only a *Perfecti* could welcome another, which meant the line from one to the next stayed unbroken back to the time of the apostles and Christ. How special. And wonderful. She bent down and bestowed the kiss of peace on a dry cheek. "You are now one of us."

The husband knelt beside the bed, holding his wife's hand.

Crying.

She retreated to the front room and prepared to leave.

Her work done.

Chapter 9

Cassiopeia was impressed with Beláncourt's plane, one of his company's private jets, outfitted in the same caramel tinted leather from his office. True to his word, the aircraft had been waiting in Lyon at eight a.m. The ride through smooth, warm air had taken less than an hour and, when the plane landed at a tiny landing strip near Lavelanet, Beláncourt was waiting for her.

"I trust you had a pleasant ride?" he asked.

"It would be hard not to."

He smiled. "It's one of our premier products. About forty million euros, fully outfitted. Should I reserve you one?"

She smiled at his attempt at charm. "Maybe two."

He laughed. "From what I'm told, you could afford them both." He motioned. "I have a car."

They walked toward a black Mercedes sedan and he opened the front passenger door for her, then slipped in behind the steering wheel. She was surprised at no chauffeur, but assumed privacy was the theme for this day.

She was familiar with the west Ariège department, the land abutting the Spanish border, where rivers cascaded out of the Pyrenean foothills forming magnificent valleys. She loved Foix, a jewel of a town, tucked between two of those rivers, crowned by an ancient chateau high on a hill. The counts of Foix once ruled the area who, along with the counts of Toulouse and Carcassonne, defended the Cathars during the Albigensian Crusade. But Simon de Montfort, who led the pope's crusade, vowed to *make the Rock of Foix melt like fat and grill its master in it.* He failed. Four times. But he did burn the town beneath the castle to the ground.

"Why are we here?" she asked.

"To show you something that may help clarify matters. I've found that seeing is much more powerful than mere explaining."

"Are you always so cryptic?" she asked.

"I'm afraid so. My Catholic upbringing, perhaps. But I've always believed that when our curiosity and sense of wonder are doubly engaged, we are more willing to entertain the fantastic. Even the preposterous."

"I'm more interested in your attack on my family business. And all over a rather unimportant Book of Hours. Hardly a valuable religious treasure. There are hundreds of them still in existence."

"Ah, that's where you are wrong. There is only one like the book you found."

A fact she realized, but she was trolling, slow and careful, trying to widen her net, hoping to snag a morsel or two of information. But she'd already allowed him to set the ground rules for the day, so she might as well enjoy the ride. She had to admit, she was curious as to what this man was up to.

"Do you know much about the Cathars?" he asked.

Actually, she did. A medieval religious sect that believed in duality. They claimed Satan was the creator of the physical world and everyone was trapped inside his evil universe, awaiting death and an ascent to heaven, where the good God reigned. They prided themselves on sacrifice, living ascetic lives, swearing off meat, wine, possessions, and children. All to free themselves of the world's temptations. The goal? To become so pure that, when they left their mortal coil, God would welcome them with open arms.

She told him what she knew.

"The idea of two gods, one good, the other evil, smacked the Catholic Church right in the face," he said. "The Cathar's God of Good was the God of the New Testament, the creator of the spiritual realm. For them, the God of Evil, Satan, was the God of the Old Testament. To a Cathar, human spirits were genderless angels, trapped in the material realm of the God of Evil, destined to be reincarnated over and over until they achieved salvation through the *Consolamentum*, which would allow them to finally become *Perfecti* and be with the God of Good. That's why they were so unafraid of death. In fact, they welcomed it since the physical world meant nothing to them."

She knew the history of what happened. How many were slaughtered? Best estimate? Around twenty thousand. Nothing short of genocide. What happened at Béziers, on July 21, 1209, seemed typical. The city was besieged and two orders were given to its inhabitants. The Catholics were to come out and leave, and the Cathars were to surrender. Neither group obeyed. The city fell the following day and all of the buildings were burned to the ground. Then the entire population—men, women, and children—was rounded up. When his men asked how to distinguish between Cathar and Catholic the crusader's commander simply said, *Kill them all. God will know his own.*

And they did.

"The Cathars never stood a chance," he told her. "The invaders were highly motivated. First and foremost there was the matter of all their sins being forgiven. Quite a gift for the medieval mind. Then there was the land grab. The crusade was a way to wipe out the local nobles and extend French power all the way to the Pyrenees. But it also made the papacy more dependent on the French kings, which eventually led to the Vatican's Avignon exile."

Which lasted nearly eighty years. Seven popes ruled from France during the 14th century, never setting foot inside the Vatican. It took a great ecumenical council in 1417 to resolve the civil war.

They kept driving through the lovely countryside, the day bright and sunny.

"I'll try not to bore you with too many details," he said. "But there are some things about the Cathars that I'd like you to understand."

Keeping him talking was the whole idea of her being there. "Please, feel free to tell me what you like."

"I want to say that I'm sorry for the legal difficulties I inflicted on your company. I can fix it all with one telephone call. But I had to get your attention and make you understand the seriousness of my offer."

He took a curve in the road and, as they came around the bend, a verdant green valley, ringed with mountains, came into view.

"All of this land was once owned by Cathar nobles," he said.

Including, as she'd already surmised, where they were headed.

The Castêl de Montségur.

Mountain of Safety.

A limestone *pog*, twelve hundred meters high, crowned with the ruins of a castle that, in the mid-13th century became a Cathar stronghold, occupied by passionate believers bound by a common conviction.

It became the last redoubt.

Beláncourt slowed the car as they drove through the village of Montségur. Seven hundred years ago more Cathars called it home. A single street ran through the tiny town, lined with tourist shops, a couple of inns, and a few cafés. Past a small church they continued down a tree-lined road, coming to a stop about ten minutes later in a graveled parking lot. She climbed out into the warm sun and stared up the green hill to the sheer, sand-colored mount, the high crag emerging from the trees like bone out of flesh, the ramparts stark against a cerulean blue sky.

"It's still impressive," he said to her. "After all the centuries."

Few other cars were present, the site short on visitors today. Odd for a Saturday.

"It's the most significant monument left to the Cathars' existence," he said to her. "Now it's a tourist attraction. Have you ever been to the top?"

She shook her head. Strange how she'd visited so many spots around the world, many quite obscure, but had never ventured to this one, right in her back yard.

"It's a brisk climb up," he said. "Popular among hikers."

She was having trouble reading him. He sounded both angry and nostalgic at the same time.

"You ready?" he asked.

"We're going up?"

"That's what we came for. You look like you're in great shape. It should not be a problem."

Yes, she jogged a few times a week and never shied away from long hours of physical activity at the construction site, but climbing a steep mountain trail should be interesting on her calves and challenge her aversion to heights.

She followed him across to a flight of roughhewn steps cut into the rock that started the path upward. A wooden sign in the shape of an Occitan Cross, similar to the one from the Book of Hours, welcomed them with a description of the site and an explanation about the trail. Off to one side stood a stone memorial, the *Prat dels Crémats*. Field of the Burned. She read the inscription on the stele. *Als catars, als martirs del pur amor crestian. 16 de març 1244.* The Cathars, martyrs of pure Christian love.

16 March 1244.

Holy ground.

Her curiosity level was piqued. Beláncourt had brought her here for a clear reason.

"When the castle yielded," he said to her, "surrender conditions were agreed upon. All of the people holed up in the castle were allowed to leave, except those who would not renounce their Cathar faith. Of course, none did. So a two-week truce was declared for everyone to think on the matter. They did, praying and fasting. During that time, a number of the defenders decided to join the ranks of the *Perfecti*. They received their *Consolamentum*, a baptism, bringing the total number of Cathars to around two hundred and five. Finally, on the day noted there on the memorial, March 16, everyone from the castle came down to here and died in a huge fire that had been set. They walked right into the flames, entirely on their own."

"They were true believers," she said.

"Or fools. It's hard to say which."

"Their deaths are still remembered."

He nodded. "That they are. Which does count for something."

"Why are we here?" she asked again.

"I will explain once we're at the top."

Chapter 10

Cassiopeia kept a close watch on her feet, making sure each step landed on solid ground. The loose soil and pebbles were a challenge. The rocky path wound up the cliff face through stands of cypress and pine, fragrant in the spring air. The wind steadily increased, blowing with more gusto the higher they climbed. Viewing stops had been created at points along the way and they lingered at one that offered a panoramic view of the forests below. Above them, the castle loomed ferocious and unwelcoming. Almost threatening. As if warning her not to come closer. The mountain's sheer power and height had surely proved the citadel's best defense. Bringing a fully equipped army up here would have been nearly impossible. No wonder a siege mentality had prevailed.

Beláncourt stayed quiet on the climb and she remained wary of his every word. She was only here out of necessity since placating him seemed the fastest route to removing the pressure on her company. She owed the over ten thousand employees that their jobs stayed secure. She owed her parents that the family concern would be protected. She owed history to make sure the book she'd found was preserved.

It took about forty-five minutes, but they finally reached their destination. Her legs had handled the strain just fine. The castle itself was simple in design. A single postern, a massive keep, walls reinforced by limestone rock surrounding a long central courtyard. It all seemed icy cold, nearly corpselike.

"This is not the original Cathar stronghold," he said. "Everyone who comes here thinks that it is, and the locals and guidebooks don't do much to discourage that. This is a 17th century French fortification that was destroyed during a war. The original Cathar castle was razed to the ground after the surrender."

He led her toward an opening in the towering wall. The wind whipped with no mercy, rushing across them as if angry. Scattered clouds overhead cast shadows on the ruins. Once inside, the wind was blocked, offering a feeling of protection, but also one of isolation as nothing could be seen past the stone. A few other visitors had braved the climb and were enjoying the ambiance.

"Do I learn why we are here now?" she asked.

"I'm after a treasure."

Why was she not surprised? "This is about gold or jewels?"

He grinned. "There is endless speculation about this particular treasure. Gold and jewels are but two of the possibilities."

Now she was curious.

"Popular culture, particularly in books—some obscure, some worldwide bestsellers—have assigned all sorts of explanations to what the Cathar treasure might be," he said. "Many believe it to be the Holy Grail. But that's nonsense. The Cathars could not have cared less about the cup of Christ." He paused. "That just makes for great stories tourists love to hear. The most mystical believers think the treasure was a text that explained an alchemical secret for how to turn base human instincts into pure and holy good. The kind that would bring spiritual enlightenment to men for all time. Sounds wonderful, doesn't it?"

That it did.

"But that's nonsense too," he said. "Follow me."

He led her from the enclosed space of ruins through a doorway in the wall. They stood on a precipice, staring across a valley, green as emerald, to peaks on the horizon that eventually joined the Pyrenees. Patches of light swept across the hillsides. Above, a hawk rode the warm currents. The breeze whipped her hair. She wanted to stretch out her arms and ride the wind too. Weightless. Free of the burden of being locked to the land. Where the other side of the *pog* was climbable, this side dropped in a sheer fall of over a thousand meters. Heights were not her thing. She tried to avoid them but had found that a challenge. Planes and helicopters were bad enough. Tall buildings, worse. Here, she was standing on solid ground, which helped, but she had no desire to venture too close to the edge. Interestingly, no barriers existed to block any approach. An easy matter to leap right off.

"Spectacular view, isn't it?" he said.

Yes, it was.

The height and vista seemed to energize Beláncourt. His face was more alive than she'd yet seen.

"There is a more rational approach to what the treasure might be," he said.

She dropped her backpack and removed two bottles of water.

They both drank long swallows.

"This was a nearly impregnable fortress," he said. "The original building rose three stories. The area around the central courtyard, where we just were, housed workshops, storage rooms, and stables for horses and mules. The inhabitants here were able to hold out for ten months in a siege, against an entire crusader army below. With your knowledge of medieval architecture, can you visualize how it might have looked all those centuries ago?"

Her mind had already made that analysis. "It would have taken years to build a stone fortress this high up, considering the path we just hiked. The rock would have been hewn out of the ground, then brought here and laid in place. Tough enough in the 17th century, when this version was erected, the difficulties in the 13th century would have been formidable. It's quite astonishing that any of it still stands."

"Not only standing," he said, "but still holding onto its secrets." He swept his arms out at the wide panorama. "The crusaders had the other side of the hill covered. Their armies were all up the path toward the fortress. No way to go up or down. But here, on this side, where there is nothing but a sheer drop down, there were no sentries. Just a few troops in the woods below to guard the base. That information we know from crusader accounts that have survived. I told you there was a two-week lull between the surrender and when the Cathars came down to die. That's the critical time, when something happened."

She waited.

Then listened.

Chapter 11

ARNAUT KNELT UNDER THE FLICKERING LIGHT OF TORCHES, HIS FACE *drawn with fatigue, his eyes glowing with anticipation. The council of elders remained silent, sitting in a circle on the hard ground, drifting in and out of meditation as if of one mind. He, too, bowed his head in prayer.*

"You are Arnaut," the senior Perfecti *said. "Who loves the wind, and chases the hare with the ox, and swims against the torrent."*

He liked that description.

"You have been chosen," the older man said. "Now it is time for you to leave."

He lifted his head but stayed on his knees. The other men rose from the circle and gathered around him. He'd lived in the mountains his entire life and knew the forests, glacial tunnels, and caves better than any of the others. He was also utterly trustworthy and devoted to his faith, all of which had made him the perfect choice.

He'd been among the first group to settle the pog *of Montségur. A place to be free of the papists, to meditate, to be safe. An eagle's nest, where an enemy could be seen approaching from every direction. The lord of Foix himself had allowed them to fortify the mount with a citadel and construct a village at its base. They came under his protection, which had brought the wrath of the crusaders who'd burned Foix to the ground. Now an army was camped below, soldiers occupying the hillside up toward the fortress, the whole site under siege.*

"We will eventually go down," the senior Perfecti *said. "We have all decided to leave this world. But not right away. We will provide you the time needed to accomplish your task."*

"I prefer to join you and the rest."

And he meant it.

"That is not possible. It is important to all of us that you be successful."

He wanted to argue but knew the effort would be useless. The decision had been made and there would be no retreat.

The older man walked over to a crevice in the stone wall and lifted a small gold casket, bringing it closer. Two of the other Perfecti approached and tied the vessel to his spine, across his chest, hard and tight, as one would secure a pack to a trusted stallion.

Which was how he felt.

The senior Perfecti stood over him and bestowed a blessing. Then the older man said, "You recall all of the instructions you've been given?"

He nodded.

"Perform them, exactly as told."

Another nod.

He was helped to his feet. One of the others presented him a cloak and a satchel of provisions, which were also tied to his body. Then the torches were extinguished and he was led from the fortress to the west wall of the mount. A black abyss lay below, studded with jagged peaks sharp enough to pierce a man's lungs. A rope had already been tied that dropped down to a point where the rocks could then be descended by hand. The air was chilly, the night brisk on his bare face and hands. In daylight the descent would be difficult. But in the pitch of night? Could he make it to the bottom?

The senior Perfecti drew close in the dark and whispered a final thought in his ear. Then the older man placed the kiss of peace on his brow. "May God be with you."

"And you, as well."

"Our fate is decided. Yours remains to be seen."

He made it to the bottom.

By the grace of God.

The climb down had taken longer than he'd thought. The moon had been high in the sky when he began but was now much closer to the western horizon. Dawn was not far away, but night still enveloped him. He'd carefully felt his way down the cliff. The first signs of meltwater had trickled the rock face and made the going even more treacherous. The rope had taken him only part of the way. The rest had been thanks to his own strength and determination.

He'd prayed the entire way.

Twice he'd slipped, sending scree into the blackness.

Which might alert one of the patrols.

Luckily, no one had noticed.

One last time, he glanced up at the fortress. Invisible in the night. All of the people who meant anything to him were there.

Would he ever see them again?

Two weeks had passed.

He'd made it away from Montségur without incident. Another reason he'd been chosen was his ability to navigate the woodlands, night or day, with confidence and agility. He'd followed the instructions he'd been given precisely. No exceptions. Going north where the Perfecti had told him to go, beyond the reach of the crusaders, and leaving the gold casket.

Now he'd returned to Montségur.

The sun had risen two hours ago and the crusaders' camp seemed abuzz with activity. It remained where they'd first pitched their tents and unhitched the trundle wagons of their whores. He'd listened from the top, night after night, to the roll of their drums, the shrill wails of their flutes, and the cries of feasting, drinking, and wenching. A similar buzz seemed evident now. So he found a position at a distance, behind one of the thick poplars, where he could observe. Reclimbing the mount to the citadel would be impossible, and he'd known that when he left.

His was to be a one-way mission.

He should have stayed where he'd gone.

But something had drawn him back here.

A new structure stood off to one side, not there two weeks ago. A large pyre. Raised, with wood stacked beneath it, like for a fire. Curiously, it was surrounded by a palisade with an open gate in front. From the woods at the base of the pog, *where the trail up began, a line of people emerged. One after the other. Men, women, children. Walking in solemn procession. One of the soldiers approached the pyre with a torch and lit the wood beneath, which caught quickly in the dry, late-winter air, forming a raging blaze.*

And when they caught the souls of my people, they gave life to their souls. And they violated me among my people, to kill souls which should not die and to save souls alive which should not live.

He finished uttering the sacred words and cursed the God of Evil for making sure he'd returned at this moment. But he thanked the God of Good for what was about to happen.

The line of believers stopped at the open gate in the palisade. He recognized all of them. They'd come down, just as the senior Perfecti *had said. That old man led the line, his head bowed, hands folded at his waist.*

Two men approached the Perfecti, *both of whom he recognized. The Governor of Carcassonne and the Bishop of Narbonne.*

They spoke to the old man, who slowly shook his head. Then he entered the palisade and, with no hesitation, stepped into the flames. One by one the others each shook their heads and followed him. He knew what they were being asked.

Do you renounce your faith?

None did.

Once all were inside the palisade the gate was closed.

The air became rank with spiraling black smoke. The stench of burnt flesh, blood, entrails, and hair filled his nostrils. The reality of what he was seeing sent him to his knees.

Grief overwhelmed him.

He stared up at the summit of Montségur and considered joining his compatriots, taking his place as another burnt offering to the now conquered citadel. But the words of the Perfecti, *whispered into his ear before he descended the mount, echoed in his mind.*

"Go with God, my son. Be safe. Bear witness to our memory so that fifty, a hundred, or five hundred years from now we will be known."

Cassiopeia listened to Beláncourt finish the story.

"As I told you below, two hundred and five died that day. That is a fact. But the *Story of Arnaut?* That's a matter of dispute. Did someone manage to escape the mount? And carry away a treasure?" He shrugged. "It's possible, but that would have been a hell of a descent."

They still stood on the western edge, precisely where the Cathar Arnaut would have begun his climb down.

"And whether that same Cathar managed to return two weeks later at the precise time of the mass execution?" he said. "That's a bit improbable too. The best guess is that the story I just told you is a composite from several people, passed down through the centuries as the tale of one."

"How did you learn it?"

He chuckled. "I was told by someone who was in a position to know."

"That's quite vague."

"I realize that. Let's leave it there, for now. The Cathars, though, did not fare well after Montségur. The Inquisition kept hunting and torturing them for confessions. They were burned at the stake, their houses and lands seized. By the 14th century they were all but gone. The last known *Perfecti*, a man named Guilhèm Belibaste, was burned at the stake in 1321. But not before saying something quite prophetic. *Al cap dels set cent ans, verdajara lo laurel.*"

The laurel will flourish again in 700 years.

"By the time Belibaste roasted," he said, "thanks to the Albigensian crusade the Languedoc had been absorbed into France, the whole region under Paris' control, the Catholic Church back in total command."

"What did he mean by *the laurel will flourish again?*"

"In Christianity, the laurel symbolizes resurrection. I suppose he means the Cathars would rise again. I have to say, I thought the whole story a myth. But it may now have been proven true, thanks to the emergence of the gold casket and book you found."

"Hence your interest?"

He nodded. "Precisely."

"The story says Arnaut went north from Montségur. Where exactly?"

He shrugged. "No one knows. But Givors is north. The fortress there at the time may have been his destination. It lay just outside what was then regarded as Cathar territory. So it would have been safe from crusaders. All we know now is that the casket was there for you to find."

"So the book inside is the treasure?"

He did not answer her. Instead, he stared off into the distance at the trees below, only the wind passing between them.

"There are Cathars today who still come here and hold vigils," he said. "They claim the stones seep the spirits of their ancestors."

"I thought Catharism was a dead religion."

"There are converts who continue to carry the mantle."

"Are you one of them?"

He shook his head. "I am a practicing Roman Catholic. To me, a Cathar is a heretic."

An interesting choice of words for the 21st century.

"You approve, then, of the massacre?"

He frowned. "Your point?"

"Heretics were burned."

"Centuries ago. Not anymore."

This man did not like to answer questions. So she asked again, "Why are we here?"

"I wanted you to see and feel what that man long ago risked his life to protect. I believe *The Story of Arnaut* to be true, and the book you found holds the key to proving that. It's a map. What the Cathars called *Le Camin de Lutz*. The Path to Light. But it's only decipherable if you know what to look for."

"And you do?"

"I know someone who does."

She said nothing.

He faced her. "I want you to know that I am not some treasure hunter. This is not about wealth. Finding whatever there is to find is a deeply personal quest of mine. I do not want to share more than that with you, or anyone for that matter. Just know that finding this is important to me."

She could see that he was being truthful.

"I respect your privacy, as to your motives," she said. "But my company is still under attack."

He said nothing.

So she tried, "I'm also assuming that the book I found is a conduit for the location of the treasure?"

He nodded.

"The elders sent Arnaut off with the Book of Hours, inside the gold casket, so it would be safe. They knew where it was secreted. Arnaut knew. But no one else." He paused. "I'm hoping you will reconsider and sell me the book. If you don't, I assure you, what I've done so far to *Terra* is just the beginning. Things will become much worse for your company. And you will have an enemy."

A smile of contempt formed on his lips.

"One that can destroy things as easily as they are built. So I urge you to carefully consider the situation before dismissing me again."

Chapter 12

THE *PERFECTI* SAT IN A CAFÉ.

She'd driven from Toulouse south to Mirepoix, about an hour's journey, to clear her head. She'd almost been caught at Vitt's chateau. But the risk had to be taken. She should have confronted the man on the ground and tried to retrieve the book, but the look in his eye had signaled she would not have been successful.

Better to retreat and regroup.

Formulate another plan.

But what?

She loved Mirepoix. Once a Cathar center, home to a cluster of *Perfecti* in the 13th century. The town's lord, Roger de Mirepoix, had been a believer. Here was where six hundred Cathars had convened a great council and commissioned the writing of a great manuscript.

La Vertat.

The Truth.

They'd also asked another local lord if they could rebuild the fortress at Montségur, a decision that led to its construction, occupation, eventual capture, and the sacrifice of its inhabitants.

The town continued to exude a medieval feel. Its arcaded main square was surrounded by sagging wooden arches, topped by half-timbered houses. St. Maurice's Cathedral had stood since the 14th century, just after the suppression of the Cathars, when the papists retook control. This was one of her favorite places in the Ariège, home to a mere three thousand people, forty-one of which were currently believers.

Flowers bloomed everywhere in planters, baskets, and climbing trestles, the air fragrant with pollen. She sat near the old magistrate's house, the wooden beams supporting the upper structure carved with tragic faces, bearded men, alligators, and tortoises. Her lunch consisted of a stew with carrots and beans in a thick broth. Normally, it also included sausage. But she'd not eaten meat in over two decades. She stared at the bowl, steam rising from its surface, her mind at a loss as to how to proceed.

Theft had failed. Normally, she'd simply wait and try again. But the presence of Roland Beláncourt urged a speedier approach. He was *her* papist. *Her* crusader trying to interject himself into something where he did not belong. The world seemed no different now than it had centuries ago. Threats still existed. Danger surrounded. People did not understand. All the Good Ones ever wanted was to live a life free of constraints, dedicated to peace, preparing themselves for an eventual final death and a welcomed release to the God of Good.

Catholics venerated the Old Testament. But the God of the Old Testament was not the God of Good, or the God of Light. Instead, He was ignorant, cruel, bloodthirsty, and unjust. The God of Evil, of Darkness. That contradiction could not be ignored.

Papists attached great value to material things. Look at their churches and cathedrals. Cardinals, bishops, priests, and popes had always lived in great luxury. They knew no other god but money and had a purse where their hearts should be. Eight hundred years ago they'd been a laughingstock. Even more so today, considering the scandals that had rocked the priesthood worldwide. Matthew 6:24 was correct. *No man can serve two masters, for either he will hate one and love the other, or else he will hold to one and despise the other.*

Catholics also idolized saints and venerated the cross. Matthew again said it best. *Watch out for the false prophets who come to you in the guise of lambs, when within lurk voracious wolves. Only their fruit will tell them apart.*

Enduring a physical life on this Satan-run earth was truly hell. Creating another life, having a child, a son or daughter who would have to do the same, seemed nothing short of cruel. Why doom an innocent to such unhappiness? As was written long ago, and as she preached to the believers—*Be chaste of body. For men and women observing the vow and way of life of this sect are in no way soiled by the corruption of debauchery. Whence, if any of them, man or woman, happens to be fouled by fornication, if convicted by two or three witnesses, he forthwith either is ejected from their group or, if he repents, is reconciled by the imposition of their hands, and a heavy penitential burden is placed upon him as amends for sin.*

A tempered mercy for weak souls.

She was not married, nor had she ever birthed a child. Many of her believers had likewise come to exercise great restraint when it came to children. Sex was tolerated, so long as it did not result in a pregnancy. Thankfully, science now provided many ways to avoid that result. Some good. Some horrible. Eight hundred years ago, only celibacy was one hundred percent effective.

She loved all of her believers. No people had ever been more humble. None more assiduous in prayer. More constant under persecution. None made more insistent attempts to lead a good life. The gospels were their only guide. Their celibacy and austerities those of a monastic ideal. Their criticism of the orthodox clergy no more severe today, or back then, than that of other puritans and reformers.

Yet they alone had been targeted for extinction.

Her religion was just as old as Catholicism, tracing back to the prophet Mani, who lived in Persia during the 3rd century. Those teachings spread from Turkey, to Bulgaria, into Italy, and later to Spain and France. She'd spent the better part of her life studying every aspect of Catharism. Sadly, little firsthand information still existed since the papists, while exterminating every believer they could find, also destroyed every text.

That was why the Book of Hours was so important.

It led to The Truth.

No doubt existed in her mind that hell was right here on earth. The evil God filled every moment of life with pain. Satan worked to confine all souls to an earthly prison. But the good God imbued people with knowledge of heaven and a divine spark that provided the ability to resist Satan and earn a way into His eternal realm. When a believer died without having experienced the *Consolamentum,* the unsaved released soul was immediately attacked by the physical world. Desperate to escape that suffering, the soul would attach to whatever host, or *lodging of clay*, that could be found. Either human or animal. No matter. Being reborn meant being given a chance to live again. Hopefully better. To finally get it right. To lead the life the good God intended and experience the *Consolamentum,* earning the right to at last be released and finally go home to heaven. Her job, as *Perfecti*, was to make that joy happen. The old woman she'd baptized last night may have already found the light, her cycle of pain ended.

Or at least she hoped so.

Eventually, her time to die would come too. And she would welcome her eternal reward. Provided she remained observant, benevolent, righteous, and kept thinking like a person surrounded by enemies.

And she was.

What better way to end her cycle of life in this physical world than return to the Cathars that which was most precious?

The Truth.

No better way at all.

Her soup seemed ready to eat. Little steam was now condensing. She lifted the spoon.

How could she accomplish such a lofty goal?

The answer seemed to be in prayer.

Where she hoped the God of Good would provide a way.

Chapter 13

CASSIOPEIA ENDED THE CALL TO HER CORPORATE HEADQUARTERS. There'd been no change in the legal situation. She'd told Beláncourt yesterday afternoon, right before she boarded his jet and returned to Givors, that he had twenty-four hours to end his litigious attack. Otherwise, there would be no more discussions between them and she would fight whatever battle he brought her way. In the car, on the drive away from Montségur, he'd tossed out a compromise. *If you will not sell, would you consider allowing me to examine the book, under your supervision, and take some photos?*

A compromise.

But she'd made it clear again that he would have to end the legal blackmail before she would even consider such a move.

It was nearing eleven a.m. and she'd spent three hours online researching the Cathars and any supposed "treasure." Everything she'd found involved either gold, silver, the Holy Grail, or some other absurd, esoteric conclusion. Nothing realistic, and Beláncourt had refused to tell her more about what he considered the treasure to be, only that the book she'd found was a path to it. Despite his arrogance and hostility, she was intrigued by the man. But, like Cotton always said, *don't run in until you know the lay of the land.*

The Book of Hours lay on the desk before her.

Thousands of similar books had been produced between the 13th and 18th centuries, many of which survived in libraries and museums. In fact, more books of hours were made than any other type. The bestseller of its day. No two were exactly alike, although they all shared one group of devotions. A set of prayers, in eight sections, meant to be said at regular intervals throughout a twenty-four-hour day. The practice of praying at multiple times came from the Divine Office, a liturgy chanted in monasteries where monks gathered for prayer on a strict daily schedule. The Book of Hours simply allowed the general public to partake of those practices. Some of the greatest paintings of the late Middle Ages and early Renaissance were not on church or museum walls. Instead, they shined forth from the pages of books like the one before her. But what made this one so special?

While reading the various online articles about the Cathars, one name kept appearing.

Simone Forte.

She was currently involved with an archeological dig near Carcassonne. Forte held a doctorate and taught medieval religion at the Université de Toulouse. When the professor's name was Googled the hits showed that she was widely regarded as one of the leading authorities on Catharism. There were numerous academic papers available. A check of the university's website provided an email address and contact number. A quick look on Amazon revealed that Simone Forte had written three books, which were all available in e-format. So she downloaded them. Two were geared for a more learned audience. The third seemed for the masses. *The Cathar Tragedy*. Published twelve years ago. Not a long volume. Only one hundred thirty-one pages. She scrolled through it on the screen and noticed the table of contents. Its five sections dealt with the people, places, and events of the Cathars. She was about to skim through and read a little when she came to the dedication page.

To my husband, Roland Beláncourt,
who makes the present wonderful
and provides the support needed to search the past.

She opened a new window on the laptop and immediately typed Roland Beláncourt and Simone Forte into the search engine.

Only four hits emerged.

Strange, given Beláncourt's public persona, but consistent with his jealous guarding of his privacy. During her previous search of only his name a few days ago, nothing had been mentioned except generic references to a former wife.

She opened all four sites.

Three seemed a rehash of the fourth, which she read in its entirety. All two paragraphs of it.

Forte and Beláncourt had been married for eleven years, the union annulled by the Archbishop of Toulouse ten years ago. There'd been no children. Interesting an annulment instead of divorce. But perhaps Beláncourt, a devout Catholic, as the article noted, had not wanted to risk excommunication, since divorce was still frowned upon by the Church. A snide comment alluded to the fact that annulments were traditionally granted for only unconsummated unions, but they were also available to the wealthiest Catholics who could afford to pay the price of permission.

She'd originally intended on e-mailing Professor Forte seeing if the woman might be interested in helping her with the Book of Hours. Now, talking to the woman no longer seemed optional. She reached for the cell phone and tapped in the number for the university. Her call was routed to the Humanities Department and Forte's office. Incredibly, someone was there, given it was a Sunday, and a young research assistant was most helpful, explaining that the professor was not on campus today, nor would she be for the next week.

"She's in Carcassonne. At the Hôtel de la Cité."

Chapter 14

THE AÉROPORT DE CARCASSONNE SAT WEST OF TOWN, A BUSTLING HUB with flights due in today, Cassiopeia noticed, from Ireland, England, Scotland, and several cities in France. She'd ended the call to Simone Forte's office and immediately chartered a plane out of Lyon that flew her three hundred kilometers south in less than two hours. By two p.m. she was on the ground and headed into the city thanks to a rental car agency.

The Cité de Carcassonne was one of the last remaining walled cities left in the world, perched where the River Aude made a sharp right turn toward the sea. Its ramparts were composed of two concentric walls with a widow's walk atop, protected by merlons and battlements, all flanked by defensive towers. Its Castle of the Counts, located inside the walls, came reinforced with a deep moat, becoming a citadel within a citadel.

The town's medieval feel had been carefully preserved with narrow winding streets, half-timbered façades, and small open squares that spread out from once active wells. A lower town outside the walls bowed to modernity, but it was the old world within, home to about seven hundred, that drew tens of thousands each year to visit. A World Heritage site. She smiled at that designation knowing the trouble Cotton had caused at several of those around the globe. She wondered what he was doing. She should call him. But first things first. She needed to speak with Simone Forte.

The Hôtel de la Cité carried the reputation as the best in town. It occupied the old neo-Gothic bishop's palace, adjacent to the basilica, offering five-star accommodations. She'd stayed there twice. Inside, she learned that the professor was on the other side of town. Which would not be a long journey given the whole place was an irregular oval, curved at the north, pointed at the south, only five hundred meters long and about half that wide.

She left the hotel and navigated the cobbled streets.

The town dated back to the first century, when it was a remote Roman settlement. Charlemagne invaded seven hundred years later and claimed control. It was captured during the Albigensian Crusade by Simon de Montfort, who eventually erected the outer walls and provided its iconic appearance. During the 19th century, her hero, Eugène Viollet-le-Duc, one of the founders of historic conservation, undertook a massive restoration project. Her master's thesis had been on Viollet-le-Duc focusing on his preservation of medieval architecture. That the city had once been a hotbed for the heretics had not been germane to her studies then.

But it was today.

Tourists were everywhere. A busy Sunday. The shops, many tucked into the alcoves that once sold necessities, now peddled souvenirs. She found her destination near the north wall. A red banner, attached to the front wall above an awning, read in gold letters *Musée de l'inquisiton*. A mannequin, dressed in medieval garb, added more camp to the local museum of torture.

She stepped inside and introduced herself, saying she would like to speak with Simone Forte. The young man excused himself and disappeared behind a curtain that guarded the start of the exhibits. A few moments later a slim woman, maybe in her late forties, early fifties, with beautiful green eyes and a face that bore few marks of life, appeared. Her blonde hair was drawn tight into a bun and a pair of bifocals sat perched on the tip of her nose. She wore an expensive black pantsuit with a crisp white blouse. Cassiopeia recognized the face from the photo in the books and introduced herself.

The older woman shook her offered hand with a firm grip.

"A pleasure to meet you, *Mademoiselle* Vitt. I've admired your restoration project for many years."

She was surprised that the connection had been made. "I appreciate you noticing. You should come see it some time."

"I would love that."

The soft voice was like honey and carried an even tone, not

ıncommon for academics. But it also signaled all business.

"Is there a place where we could speak in private?" she asked. "I've come to show you something."

"Now that's rather mysterious. But, yes, we can talk in the back. I've been utilizing a room here as my field lab. I'm working with some archeologists who are digging not far from here. The owner of this museum is a friend and offered the space."

She followed the woman into the museum.

A few visitors roamed inside.

"Despite the tourist flavor," Forte said, "the exhibits are reasonably authentic. The dioramas are quite realistic, while the mannequins, God bless them, leave a bit to be desired."

The place was reminiscent of a wax museum, but with added macabre touches like what appeared to be dried blood on the floor in one room and some entrails in another. Deeper in she saw a Judas chair made of nails which, a sign noted, was used primarily on witches. A hell cage hung from the ceiling, inside of which prisoners were once left naked in the elements until they died. A stretching ladder and breaking wheel, one to dislocate the limbs, the other to snap bones, sent a chill through her. In a long-vaulted gallery were axes, chastity belts, and old maniacal-looking medical instruments. At its far end, inside a low archway, hung an oak door.

"Here we are," Forte said, inserting a skeleton key.

The room beyond was square with a window to the outside. After the dim light of the museum, it took a moment for her eyes to adjust to the sunlight. A roughhewn rectangular table filled the space, upon which lay a slab of rock.

"My workshop," she said.

She admired the stone on the table. "Is this Cathar?"

The professor nodded. "I believe so. The carving was found at a dig near here."

The slab was about a meter long and half that wide. Upon its face was the clear hewn image of a dove, carved all the way through.

"It may have come from Montségur," Forte said. "We know from other accounts that the site was looted after the Cathars surrendered and the citadel was razed. This particular style is common in that region. The dove was the Cathars' most powerful symbol."

Cassiopeia found her phone and brought up several images of the Book of Hours that she'd taken earlier. Some of the cover, some inside, a few of the casket itself. "I have something else that may be Cathar. This was found at my construction site six days ago."

She handed over the phone.

Forte studied each one with close scrutiny, then asked, "How many pages are in the book?"

"Seventy-three, all illustrated."

Using two fingers, Forte enlarged the images to fill the phone's screen and studied them again. Cassiopeia watched the other woman carefully, noting how she perused each with a careful examination.

Forte handed the phone back. "This is quite a find."

"In what way?"

"Where is the book?"

Not an answer to her question. "Safe at my estate. We had a robbery attempt, and a private collector is pressuring me to either sell the book to him or allow him to examine it."

"May I inquire who?"

"Your ex-husband."

A look of shock filled Forte's face. "Roland?"

She nodded. "It's another reason why I'm here. Not only are you a recognized expert, but you also know him. I was hoping you might be able to tell me his real interest. He says it's a conduit to a Cathar treasure of some sort. The Path to Light."

"You've spoken to Roland?"

"Twice."

Forte stepped around to the far side of the table, opposite from her. The stone slab, with the dove, lay between them.

"*Mademoiselle* Vitt—"

"Cassiopeia. Please."

"Then I'm Simone."

She nodded in acceptance of the courtesy.

"My ex-husband is a most complex man. He and I have had little contact for the past decade. We said all there was to say when our marriage ended."

"Interesting how a marriage that lasted for eleven years could be annulled."

"Yes, it is. But the explanation is intensely personal and has nothing to do with you or your book."

She accepted the rebuke with grace. She'd pushed to see how far she might be able to go, which had not been much. "I apologize. But I'm in investigatory mode, which makes me a bit nosey at times."

"Quite understandable. And if you've engaged Roland twice, then you are aware of the frustration he can pose."

Most definitely.

"I watched you as you studied the photos. That book spoke to you. It means something to you."

Simone nodded. "As a scholar who has devoted the better part of her life to studying ancient religions, Catharism being one of those, what you've found could be historic."

She waited for more.

"Did he tell you *The Story of Arnaut?*"

"He did. At the top of Montségur."

"I see he's not changed. Always a flare for the dramatic. But it did probably make the story more vivid."

"Enough that I engaged in further research, which led me to you."

"The legend is that Arnaut was sent away from Montségur, right before the citadel surrendered, on a special mission. Holed up there were the last of the Cathars' *Perfecti*. The most important minds they had. They'd all climbed the *pog* and taken refuge inside the castle. Their last act was to safeguard their most sacred object."

"Which can't be monetary."

"Not in the least. It was called *La Vertat*. The Truth. A manuscript that memorialized all that it meant to be Cathar. Their bible, if you will. The only written account of the religion's beliefs. Once they realized they were not going to leave Montségur alive, they either created or modified a Book of Hours. One with a rose on its cover and many symbols inside. All written in Occitan. They called it *Le Camin de Lutz*. The Path to Light." Simone pointed at the phone. "That book."

"Belàncourt refused to tell me anything about the treasure, only that its finding was intensely personal to him. This Path to Light, is that significant?"

"Those last *Perfecti* knew the end was near. The crusaders had won. They were about to be extinguished. They wanted their religion to live on. To not die or be forgotten. Prior to ascending the mount, they hid away a special writing. *La Vertat.* Where there are many versions of the Christian Bible, printed over the centuries and translated by a multitude of people, for the Cathars there is but one, with no copies. The Truth. The Book of Hours supposedly leads the way to find that truth."

Simone Forte seemed smart, intelligent, straightforward and genuinely intrigued. She also knew Roland Beláncourt better than anyone alive. *The enemy of my enemy is my friend.* Absolutely.

"Would you like to examine the book?" she asked her.

The woman's face lit up. "It would be marvelous to have a look."

She needed answers and this source seemed the fastest way to obtain them.

"I've always thought the *Camin de Lutz* a myth," Simone said. "A story. A fable. There was no Path to Light. Which meant that there was no *La Vertat.* But what you found seems to suggest otherwise. That Cathar bible may actually be out there, waiting to be found."

"Is there any more to the legend?"

"Only bits and pieces. It is said the Cathars hid The Truth well. They did not want the crusaders to ever find it. No one has any idea where that could be. I know a few antiquity scholars who searched for a time but gave up. There is but one other clue to the location that survived the centuries."

She waited.

"*Le menarà al lac del saber.*"

She translated the Occitan.

The rose will lead to the Lake of Learning.

Chapter 15

THE *PERFECTI* STOOD ON THE RAMPARTS OF CARCASSONNE AND
watched Cassiopeia Vitt drive from the car park. She'd followed her from
the inquisition museum, imagining being with Vitt in that car, insisting
that she be allowed to have the illuminated manuscript. Holding it,
studying it, then following its lead—the Path to Light—deciphering what
had been encrypted into the illustrations and finding The Truth. Being
here, in Carcassonne, always made her think of the past. Hard not to,
considering the ambiance. Why had her religion threatened so many?
Why had it been necessary to eradicate so peaceful a people?

All sacred beliefs contrasted Light and Dark. Catholics. Protestants.
Muslims. Hindus. Buddhists. Even pagans. Cathars were no different,
striving for inner liberation, focusing on spirituality. Evil might triumph
temporarily, but sanctity always prevailed.

The Albigensian Crusade no exception.

Evil won for a moment, but at a price.

The papacy was permanently damaged by the savagery, its status
weakened, while the power of kings grew. The fanatical suppression of
fellow Christians had consequences since, if the Cathars could be silenced,
why not everyone else? Another crusade called to attack the Franks? Or
the Spanish? Or the English? Anyone who disagreed with Rome? That
fear had not gone unnoticed and the secular powers set about on a course
to dominate Rome and control its pope.

And they did.

For a long time.

She continued to watch until Vitt's car disappeared around a bend in the road. Then she descended the ramparts and walked to the count's castle, passing an endless line of shops and cafés, busy with visitors. Carcassonne's legacy stretched back to the dawn of history. Always sleepy and slow. Impregnable to all enemies, save two.

Treason and famine.

Both of which had extracted a toll.

She found the fortified castle, which contributed six towers to the outer walls, crossed the bridge-moat, paid the admission fee, then climbed a spiral staircase that wound a path up into one of the towers, a place few tourists ventured. At the top the arches opened out toward the lower city with its paved streets laid out at right angles, flat as a checkerboard, no different than a thousand other communities around France. No noise intruded from below, leaving her alone with her thoughts. She soaked in the encircling panorama of the valley beyond and the muddy River Aude. Beauty loomed in every direction beneath a cloud-flecked sky.

The Cathar message would resonate today.

She was convinced of that.

The laurel will flourish again in 700 years. That was what the great Guilhèm Belibaste had said in 1321, right before they burned him. Had that time come? Perhaps. Miraculously, the Book of Hours had appeared from the ground. Fate? A sign? Coincidence?

Hard to say.

Carcassonne had once been a formidable Cathar stronghold. Eventually, in 1209, the crusaders laid siege, forcing people to crowd into the city, seeking safety. Too many. A hot summer taxed the water supply and forced some difficult decisions. No one, Cathar or crusader, wanted to destroy the town. And there was no way the defenders could hold out. So a deal was offered. If the inhabitants surrendered, all lives would be spared, provided the people walked out wearing nothing but their shirts and breeches, carrying nothing, as one had said, *but their sins.*

And that was what happened.

Such a disgrace.

Two hundred kilometers away, in Marmande, a different result occurred. By then ten years had elapsed since the fall of Carcassonne and the crusaders had perfected their terror. No deals were offered. Five thousand died after the city was taken. Men, women, children. Lords, ladies, peasants. All stripped naked, their flesh, blood, brains, trunks, imbs, and faces hacked to pieces. Lungs, livers, and guts were tossed aside on the open ground, as if they had rained down from the sky, left for the animals. Marshland and dry earth ran red with blood. Not a soul was left alive, the town razed and set afire.

And not atypical.

She'd spent half of her life devoted to learning how to be a Cathar, communing with others of a like belief. Of course, the great paradox was that the only historical assistance came from Inquisition records, or other enemies of the religion. Not a single original Cathar text had survived. Not one. History truly was written by the victor. But there may be a chance to rewrite those lies. The Book of Hours may now be in reach.

Which could lead to The Truth.

She heard voices below, beyond the stairway.

Tourists. Exploring the castle.

She needed to leave and return to Toulouse. Only a hundred kilometers to the west. The drive would give her time to think. Time to determine what might have to be done. Unlike her ancestors, she did not intend to willfully submit to oppression. Seven hundred years had taught that the meek only get killed.

And that would not be her fate.

She would not allow this opportunity to pass.

Chapter 16

ROLAND BELÁNCOURT ENTERED THE CATHÉDRALE SAINT-ÉTIENNE. Nobody knew when the great church had first been built. Best guess was sometime during the time of Charlemagne. The present misshapen building appeared as if it had been taken apart by a child, then reassembled in the dark. A merger of two incomplete styles, one massive and powerful, the other sleek and luminous.

Dark and Light.

The heretic, the Bishop of Toulouse, had incited the locals against Rome from its pulpit. The counts of Toulouse had worshipped here which explained why, after the crusades ended the local lineage had been extinguished and a stamp of royalty placed throughout the church. That's when the fabulous Baroque altarpiece, the intricate grills, and an ensemble of magnificent stained-glass windows appeared to evidence both French and papist wealth and power.

He paraded down the center aisle, the pews filled with people who'd come for the Sunday evening mass. Most of the heads were bent in deliberation, only a collective silence binding them. He caught the stares, as some recognized him. Toulouse was the birthplace of European rockets, the Concorde, and the Airbus. The French space agency was headquartered nearby, along with the national weather service. There were countless research centers, high-tech firms, and elite training schools. He was right at the center of everything, his company a giant, owned and operated by a native son. Which these people clearly knew.

But they also needed to know he was a man of God. His allegiance to the Church and Rome. Religion mattered to him, as it should to everyone. His parents and grandparents had worshipped right here. As their grandparents before them. He'd supported this cathedral with both time and money, the local bishop a personal friend.

He took his seat and the mass began.

He knelt, along with the rest of the congregation.

The choir began its angelic rendition of *Gloria in Excelsis*.

He closed his eyes and prayed.

The priest ended the mass with a dismissal to go in peace.

Outside, the sun had receded, the stained glass windows darkening to the day. He crossed himself and rose, leaving the pew and walking toward the rear doors. He felt refreshed, like always after mass. Which was why he regularly attended. Entering the church he always kept his head bowed. Not so when leaving. And that's when he saw her. Sitting in the last pew.

Simone.

They'd had no contact in years. Odd, considering they lived in the same town. But with over a half million residents it was easy to avoid one another. She still looked lovely, a radiant face and bright eyes that concealed an unmatched intellect. An amazing woman whom he once loved. More than he ever realized. But she'd betrayed that devotion. In an unforgivable way.

He stopped and faced her.

"I need to talk to you," she said, her voice low.

Not hello, how are you, go to hell. Nothing. Just she had to talk to him. He could see little had changed.

"Certainly not here," he said.

She shrugged. "Why not? This is your sacred church. What better place?"

He caught her sarcasm. No sense arguing. The nave was rapidly emptying and he did not want a spectacle. He stepped into the pew and sat beside her but kept his face toward the altar. "What is it, Simone?"

"Leave Cassiopeia Vitt's manuscript alone."

He shook his head. "This is neither the time, nor the place, to have this conversation."

"She came to see me."

New information, but not surprising given Simone's reputation with Cathar history. So he made clear, "I'll have that manuscript."

"You hate me that much?"

"I loathe the sight of you. Just sitting here turns my stomach."

Memories washed over him in sickening waves. Horrible thoughts of horrible things. Tumultuous emotions churned inside. His eyes felt the unaccustomed dampness of a renewed grief. His body ached like an unhealed wound. But he kept calm. "I knew, at some point, you would show yourself. I didn't think it would take Vitt long to find the world's most renowned expert on heresy." He added a splash of disgust to his tone. "And even faster for her to connect you and me. You will not see that manuscript."

"I already have."

He finally glared her way. "Photos, I'm sure. Vitt's not stupid enough to remove it from her estate. Someone tried to steal it. Was that you?"

She said nothing.

"You need to see the real thing. We both know that," he told her.

The nave was now empty. Just his past remained.

He decided to be cavalier and not allow this ghost to haunt him any further. "This is it, Simone. *Le Camin de Lutz* has been found. The Path to Light. It's real." He kept his eyes locked on hers and saw she knew that too. "You will not have it. I have the means to stop you. And I will."

"Your hate will devour you."

"It already has."

He stood and walked away.

THE *PERFECTI* ENTERED ONE OF THE CATHEDRAL'S SIDE CHAPELS. Roland Beláncourt had left nearly a half hour ago. She'd lingered in the dim quiet, though she preferred a cathedral of trees and mountains over stone, wood, tapestries, and glass. Cathars had never required such trappings to affirm their faith.

Quite the contrary, in fact.

A confusion of expression surrounded her.

The church's great door off center, arches that appeared without relation to one another, a tower in no particular style, an erratic interruption of windows. But the uniqueness cast a beauty, similar to what character gave to the human countenance. Rigid regularity of features, mathematical balance, and a lineless surface made only for doll-like prettiness. A façade. A faux. Nothing special or unique. But when the features varied, the angles deviated from plumb, the surfaces became etched with significant lines, that was when there was a story to tell.

This church had a story.

Everything in its entirety, but nothing in particular.

Like herself.

High above hung the rose window.

A 12th century innovation, usually placed at the west end of a nave, near the transept ends. It had been the introduction of tracery in the 13th century that converted the mundane into spectacular. Its radiating elements consisted of an intricate network of wavy, double-curved bars, creating geometric forms and flame-like shapes. Rose windows were common throughout France.

Reims, Amiens, Notre Dame.

And here, in Toulouse.

Along with one on the cover of the Book of Hours.

She breathed in the incense-laced air. The scent brought back childhood memories when she was brought here by her parents to worship. She came to hate the stench of frankincense. The perfume of holiness and hell. Of obedience and concession. Of pomp and circumstance. But now was not the time to remember.

The time had come to act.

She'd come to gauge her enemy. To look him in the eye. But nothing had changed. Roland still despised her. He knew her as Simone Forte, a woman he'd once married. But thanks to a legal annulment their union never existed. Once they'd both been devout Catholics. He maintained his faith, but she became a Cathar, and not just in name only. How could the sanctity of Jesus Christ and all His teachings be required to be obeyed on the one hand then, on the other, the Church pillaged, murdered, raped, stole, and destroyed in His name? Being a learned woman she'd read many religious works from around the globe. Of them all dualism seemed the most logical. The Cathars the most gentle. They'd understood that in order to be good, a person had to first be kind truthful, and humble. No exceptions. No lapses. The priest who'd just said mass had worn silk robes with glittering gold thread. The bishop of this cathedral sported an episcopal ring with an amethyst the size of a walnut. And what of his gold miter studded with amethyst diamonds? What of this grand building itself, just one of thousands of Catholic temples that existed around the world as monuments to themselves?

None of that was required by the God of Good.

She felt dirty and disgusted just standing here.

Nothing she could see offered a path to heaven.

She, like every Cathar before her, wanted only to practice their faith in peace. But Roland was not going to allow that. He had a mission One fueled by hate. But it was good to know that he too had sensed that this find might be the right one. Long ago they'd talked of the Book of Hours, the Path to Light and its connection to The Truth. He knew what this discovery would mean to her. Which explained why he'd moved immediately to intervene, denying that which was precious to her to somehow lessen the pain of her denial to him.

Like her ancestors, a papist now stood in her way.

One intent on crushing her.

She turned to leave and noticed something on the floor.

A rosary.

Curled onto itself. Probably dropped by one of the worshipers. Beads on a string to count the prayers. So many. Repeated over and over.

And for what?

What had catechism taught?

With the Hail Mary we invite the Virgin to pray for us. She joins Her prayer to ours. Therefore it becomes ever more useful, because what Mary asks She always receives. Jesus can never say no to whatever His Mother asks. With your prayer, made together with Your heavenly Mother, you can obtain the great gift of bringing about a change of hearts. Each day, through prayer, you can drive away from yourselves and from your homeland many dangers and many evils.

All lies.

And unnecessary.

Another papist invention to keep the faithful close.

One the Cathars had never required.

She walked away, resolute, and made a point to plant the sole of her shoe directly atop the rosary, cracking the beads.

She was the *Perfecti*.

And, unlike her ancestors, who'd willingly walked into the flames to flee the God of Evil, she would confront the Darkness head on.

With whatever it took.

Chapter 17

CASSIOPEIA HAD MADE THE DECISION QUICKLY YESTERDAY. SHE would involve Simone Forte. If, for nothing else, her presence may irritate Beláncourt and throw him off guard, as clearly there was a history between the two.

Simone had arrived bright and early at the chateau and started working. Viktor had stayed with her, keeping an eye on the book, a precaution that the professor seemed to understand. They'd been ensconced in the lab for the past four hours, the noon hour approaching. A week had gone by since the book had been found and a lot had happened. She'd talked to Cotton several times and he'd advised caution in dealing with Beláncourt. *Get the answers before asking the questions.*

Good advice.

Which had cinched bringing Simone into the fold.

The legal attack on *Terra* had not waned, nor had Beláncourt been back in contact. She'd instructed corporate headquarters to sit tight and be patient. She was handling the problem in the most direct way possible.

Simone had brought with her an array of old maps, some dating back to the 13th century. None were hard copy originals. Instead, they were all high-resolution images on a laptop, capable of magnification down to the smallest detail. She'd also brought a chart of symbols, many of which appeared in the various illustrations inside the book, embedded in clever, nearly imperceptible, ways, looking more like art than letters.

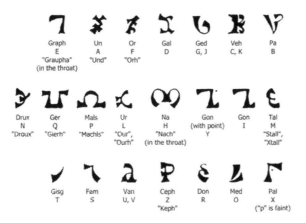

"What are these?" she asked Simone.

"The Cathars lived in dangerous times, but they still needed to communicate. So they devised their own language, one that only the *Perfecti* utilized. We know this because a sort of Rosetta Stone survived that provided a means of interpreting the symbols. It wasn't found until the early part of the 20th century. This chart was composed from that."

She studied the odd assortment of scribbles, with little rhyme or reason to their shapes. Which was probably the whole idea.

"To my knowledge," Simone said, "no one back then ever deciphered them. So the code worked. Thank goodness a means to read it survived."

Viktor was watching with intense interest. They'd found many artifacts at the construction site, but nothing like this. She'd brought him into her confidence with the condition that everything he saw and heard stayed between them. She did not want a repeat of the leak with *Nouvelles de l'art*. Shelby had been dismissed, after being non-apologetic at her clear breach of trust. And thank goodness she was gone. With Simone Forte around, the last thing she needed was an untrustworthy, nosey reporter. Also, being Monday, the construction site was closed to visitors. Another fortuitous occurrence.

"Those symbols are here," Simone said, "on every page of this book. The key, though, is the dove. It's correct on every page, head facing skyward, wings extended, similar to what you saw yesterday in my lab. Except for the twenty-sixth illustration. There, it's different. That cannot be a mere mistake."

The Book of Hours lay open on the table. Not the best way to examine its pages, but the spine was already in poor condition. She studied the page Simone had noted and saw the Cathar dove, reversed, its wings extended but its head down, buried within the margin illustrations. She counted nine birds among the symbols from the chart, all woven together in a rich, artistic pattern. She had lots of questions but did not want to share all of those answers with Viktor.

"Could you wait outside for a few minutes?" she said to him. "I'll stay with the book."

He nodded and left the lab. She loved that he never argued nor questioned, just trusted her judgment.

"I appreciate that," Simone said. "I would prefer to keep this between us."

"I agree. This is our problem."

"There may only be three people in the world who can decipher this puzzle," Simone noted. "Lucky for you, I'm one of those. I first came across *The Story of Arnaut* while working on my doctoral thesis. It's fascinated me ever since."

"I assume your ex-husband knows that?"

Simone nodded. "We often discussed the possibility that this Book of Hours existed, and its possible importance to Cathar history."

"He told me his involvement here was intensely personal."

"An understatement. Our marriage did not end well. My ex-husband hates me, and has for a long time."

"Can you tell me why?"

"I could. But I'm not."

It seemed no matter which road she took, with either Simone or Beláncourt, it led to a dead end.

"Your ex-husband doesn't have this book," she said. "We do. That gives you an advantage. Can you interpret it?"

Simone nodded. "*Le Camin de Lutz*. The Path to Light. I think I may be able to follow it."

She was listening, totally intrigued.

Simone pointed at the twenty-sixth page. Drawings filled the right margin, then angled left and spread across the top. Text filled the space framed out by the illustrations. The upside-down dove appeared at intervals, a few centimeters apart, forming a line up the outer edge that stopped about halfway across the top.

"The Cathars lived among their enemies in plain sight. They were here, but not there. I can only assume that the dove being upside down only on this page is representative of that. It's there, on every page of the book, but different on this one. Look at the illustrations on page twenty-six. The doves stop here and here."

Simone pointed to one upside-down dove at the upper left, the other a few centimeters away, right before the line of doves angled down the right edge of the page.

"Between the two stops, the symbols are no longer random. Instead they form two words. Lac. Saber."

She knew her Occitan.

Lake. Learning.

"Then, beneath is three more words. *Rosa. Bèstia roja.*"

She caught the connection to the other clue Simone mentioned yesterday.

Le menarà al lac del saber.

The rose will lead to the Lake of Learning.

But *bèstia roja*?

"What is the Red Beast?"

"I have no idea. It's new information."

"What now?" she asked.

"I need some more time with this."

Two hours later Cassiopeia returned to the lab, having been summoned by Viktor, who'd returned inside to babysit their visitor.

She entered the door to see a smile on his face.

"She's got it."

Simone seemed excited too. "I was able to link some of the words from the book to points on the ground. They correspond to a crude map of Occitania that has survived, which was what this whole region of modern France was called in the 13th century."

That she knew. The land of rebels and troubadours.

Simone directed her attention to the old map on the screen. "Here, where the River Valarties joins the Garonne, near Arties, right on the French-Spanish border, there was once a lake. It's there on the map."

She saw its outline among what appeared to be mountains and high terrain, delineated with squiggly lines. "What's that in the middle?"

"An island is my guess. Lots of lakes in the Pyrenees have small islands, high spots that weren't flooded by the water coming down from the hills. Look what the lake is called."

She'd already noticed. *Rosa.*

Rose Lake.

"It's not there anymore," Simone said, changing the image to a modern map of the same region, which showed no body of water. "It dried up. That's happened all over, as rivers alter course and glaciers in the Pyrenees shift. That may have also helped, over time, shield the location from anyone looking. But that doesn't mean there's no something there to find."

Cassiopeia smiled. "There's only one way to find out."

BELÁNCOURT STEERED THE POWERBOAT DOWN THE RIVER GARONNE, keeping a respectable speed, but taking each turn smooth and gentle. Nina St. Clair stood toward the stern and cheered as her ten-year-old son held his own on the skis. Six months ago the boy could hardly stand on them. Now he handled himself with ease. Next step? Losing one of them and trying slalom.

But not quite yet.

He came to a straightaway and glanced back, checking the boy's posture. Everything looked great. Straight spine. High shoulders. Arms extended. Knees flexing. The river seemed a bit malevolent today, increasing in strength, dragging and lunging at the boat.

"He's doing great," he shouted over the motor to Nina.

She smiled back at him and mouthed, "Thank you for this."

He shook his head. "He's a terrific kid, and I love being here."

Nina was in town for the week. She lived in Italy but visited often, many times bringing young Georges along. He'd blocked off his Monday schedule and rented the boat so they could spend some fun time together. He and Nina had dated for nearly three years. Was it going anywhere? Probably not. His self-confidence, which he knew attracted her, was more an illusion, a wafer-thin puncturable envelope around him, always threatened by the past. He fought hard to resist its effects, but there was no denying their power over him. He enjoyed her company, though, and was keeping an open mind, especially when it came to Georges. But no matter how much time he spent with the boy, how close they became, one fact was clear.

He'd never be his father.

An ex-husband would always hold that position.

Georges had been seven when they first met. Nina had introduced them and the young man had quickly extended his hand to shake, saying *nice to meet you*. He'd been immediately touched by the courtesy and the two of them had hit it off. They'd gone mountain hiking, snow skiing, and, of course, flying. Georges seemed to love planes, showing a real interest in aviation. He'd taken him through the manufacturing plant and they'd spent hours talking about flying.

The dock was rapidly approaching.

He waved for Georges to let go and swung the boat around to retrieve the boy from the river. Fifteen minutes later they were all seated on the terrace at *L'Emulation Nautique*, staring out at the river. The restaurant was a local favorite, heavy with rural ambiance. Georges enjoyed a burger and fries. Beláncourt chose the tuna tartar and Nina ordered grilled langoustines.

"Can I ski some more after lunch?" Georges asked, still high from the activity.

"If Roland has the time to take you," she said, providing an out.

Which he did not take. "We have nothing but time. Sure. I rented the boat for the entire day. I might even try the water myself."

"Does that mean I can drive?" Georges asked.

"Perhaps," he said. "With your mother's help."

They enjoyed the meal, and he savored his time with them both. He'd built some of the world's great planes, but a family was the one thing he'd never been able to create. Fate and circumstances had combined to deprive him of a child of his own. Adoption had certainly always been an option, as was a stepchild like Georges, but he'd wanted one from blood. For the Beláncourt genes to continue on.

But that would never be.

And all because of Simone.

Seeing her on Sunday had refueled his bitterness and reminded him once again that the future he wanted was absent, only the present existed.

And it was not pleasant.

They finished lunch.

He was walking back to the dock when his cell phone buzzed. He'd left specific instructions with his office that he not be bothered unless absolutely necessary. He checked the display. Not the office. Something else.

Important.

"I'll meet you at the boat," he said to Nina.

She nodded and smiled, then she and Georges headed off.

He drifted to a quiet spot near the riverbank and answered the call. "What do you have?"

"Your ex-wife came straight to Vitt's chateau this morning. She's been here ever since."

"Were you able to see or hear anything?"

"Both. The parabolic mic worked great, even though they were inside the site's field lab the whole time."

He waited.

"Simone deciphered something within the Book of Hours and determined a possible location for what she called 'the truth.'"

The exact words he'd wanted to hear.

Simone was smart. As was Vitt. Together, they'd make a formidable team. That was why he'd sent his man to follow Simone, which had led his eyes and ears straight to Cassiopeia Vitt.

"Tell me everything."

He listened to more of what Simone and Vitt had discussed.

"They're planning to travel south tomorrow to take a look," his man said.

"Do you have an exact location?"

His man gave him more of the details he'd heard.

"Do you want me to follow them tomorrow?"

"No," he said. "I'll handle that myself."

Chapter 18

CASSIOPEIA CLIMBED FROM THE VEHICLE AND ADMIRED THE EPIC wilderness. The Pyrenees extended from the Atlantic to the Mediterranean, a line of rust-stained, limestone peaks along the French and Spanish border, forming a four hundred and fifty kilometer natural wall. Pot-holed with lakes, many were secreted in high, inhospitable places with little vegetation. Springs bubbled out of nearly every hole, forming torrents and waterfalls that people came from all over the globe to enjoy.

Legend clung to these mountains. Other ranges outstripped them in height, but none in beauty and romance. Everywhere, virgin summits gleamed against the blue sky. She knew that crumbling villages lurked among the hills, many castle-topped and breathing the atmosphere of vanished centuries. The manners and customs of lost ages colored their inhabitants. Among the valleys lived tales of Charlemagne, Franks, Visigoths, Saracens, Moors.

And Cathars.

They were deep inside a French national park, the land having been publicly preserved since the 1950s. Nearly five hundred square kilometers of pristine mountainous landscape, all the way to the Spanish border. To save time, they'd flown south from Lyon in a helicopter. She'd dispatched one of her employees last evening to drive the five hundred kilometers in one of her Range Rovers, the vehicle waiting for them when they landed. That had also allowed her to send along the proper equipment they might need, based on Simone's recommendations.

Her newfound ally had spent the night at the chateau and they'd had a lovely evening, talking history and France. She seemed like an intelligent woman. The only subject that remained off limits was Roland Beláncourt. And she'd respected Simone's reluctance hoping that, at some point, she would open up about what had happened between them.

Simone stepped out into the crisp morning air.

They'd driven into the park and followed a twisting, rising road that meandered through the foothills, climbing ever steadily toward peaks that were not all that far away. Little human expression was in sight, save for the asphalt road, the view from the car park out across a long valley, flanked by protecting hills.

"I've long suspected that this area was the place," Simone said. "Where exactly? I had no idea. But I thought somewhere in these mountains would have been the perfect spot for the Cathars to hide their most precious object. What we are looking at, this particular valley, was once underwater. An alpine lake, high in the Pyrenees, called Rose."

Cassiopeia admired the high valley, rock-strewn and wild, its floor overgrown with briers, scrub oak, heather, and lavender. Towering walls of naked limestone, streaked with blue shadows, rose on three sides, the rock face bare with few cracks, crevices, or protrusions. Sure, there'd been centuries of weather and erosion, but the clear outline of what could have held a lake remained.

"Look there," Simone said, pointing. "Off to the right. The terrain rises sharply, levels off, then falls on every side. That had to be the island in Rose Lake we saw on the map."

"Have you been here before?"

Simone shook her head. "Not here. But other spots a few miles away."

They'd spent hours last night studying the illustrated manuscript, taking pictures of the pages and analyzing the maps. Simone had brought her notes from previous study, along with photos of symbols carved into rocks she'd located all across southern France. The book itself remained back at the chateau, locked in the safe, under Viktor's guard.

Their perch offered an excellent view of the magnificent scenery. No other visitors were in sight, Tuesday apparently not a busy day in this park. She allowed Simone time with her thoughts, practicing what Cotton loved to say.

Those in a hurry usually get fooled.

"Let's get our gear," she finally said.

BELÁNCOURT LOWERED HIS BINOCULARS.

He'd traveled south last evening after finishing his day with Nina and Georges. He'd enjoyed himself, relishing, if only for a few hours, in the joy of a family. Thoughts of marriage had again crept into his mind. But though he liked Nina, and he worshipped Georges, he did not love her. It had been so long since he last loved anyone that he'd simply forgotten how. Simone was right. Hate had consumed him, and every time he thought himself past it, he discovered that it was not the case. Luckily, he remained rational enough to know that loving Nina's child would not substitute for loving her. He'd keep seeing her, keep spending time with Georges, but the relationship would eventually end. A shame. But inevitable.

That's what came from a shattered heart.

One that nothing could put back together.

Earlier, he'd stopped all speculation and allowed his emotions to subside, his mind to stop questioning, resolving that the time had come to act. He stood on a ridge, about five hundred meters away from Simone and Vitt, hidden by the trees. He'd been waiting at the national park for them to arrive, his spot already staked out thanks to what his man had learned yesterday, since they'd continued to electronically monitor the conversations into the night. Now he knew that eight centuries ago the valley below him had been underwater, everything submerged save for an island in the northwest corner. That high ground remained and, somewhere near there or perhaps on it, lay the greatest treasure of the Cathar religion.

La Vertat.

The Truth.

Which meant nothing to him. It carried no value. No importance. No significance. The whole thing heretical. All that mattered was that it was important to Simone. She'd spent her life searching for it.

And now it lay in reach.

But she would not have it.

Simone followed the trail through a tangled mass of leaves and shrubs. The sun slow-baked the ground, casting hard-edged shadows, coating their arms and faces in a thin coat of perspiration. Surely the trail was popular with hikers, but not today. She and Vitt were alone.

Or were they?

Could Roland be out there? Watching? She could not underestimate his resentment. Not this time. That was why she'd brought her gun, safely tucked in her backpack, ready, just in case. She would not be led to slaughter like her ancestors.

Far from that, in fact.

They kept walking, deviating from the path, heading for the valley's northwest corner. What had once surely been a steep slope, elevating land from water, had been shaved down to a slope that descended on all sides from a small wooded promontory. They climbed the incline of soft soil and scree and crested the lip of the rock shelf. The rhythmic tapping of a woodpecker greeted their arrival. Birch, pine, and scrub were thickly sown across the shelf.

"Let's spread out and see what there is to find," Simone said.

They both dropped their backpacks and headed off in separate directions. Five minutes later she spotted a dove carved at the base of a gray boulder, its body and wings visible in the stone's discoloration. Time had eroded most of it away, but there was enough to see one thing.

The image had been prepared upside down.

She was about to call out when Vitt yelled, "I have something."

She hustled over and saw another inverted dove at the base of another boulder.

"These are carved all over this region," she told Vitt. "But none are upside down. And if you were not privy to what we know, that anomaly would not be important." She gently traced the image on the gray rock face. "We have two landmarks."

And she told Vitt about the other.

They were close. She could feel it. The Cathars had been a simple people, possessed of simple thoughts. The whole idea of their religion was to keep it simple. So this quest would not be complicated.

"I'd say my dove and yours are about twenty meters apart," Simone noted. "Mark this with something we can see, and I'll go do the same."

She hustled back and laid a branch from the ground atop the boulder. Then she fanned out and, a few minutes later, found another chunk of rock with another upside-down dove down near its base partially buried in the ground.

She'd almost missed it.

Vitt had headed off in the opposite direction. She played a hunch and called out, telling her to explore to the right of her initial find. She watched as Vitt followed the instruction.

"Come about parallel to me," she said. "But stay in a line off the first dove you found."

Vitt seemed to adjust her course. If she was right, there should be another marker near where her companion was looking.

"I have it," Vitt called out.

"Mark it where I can see it."

Vitt did and she tagged her boulder too. A quick look through the trees showed that the four doves formed a rough square, about twenty meters long on each side.

"Stay where you are," she said to Vitt.

And she hustled back to the first dove she'd found.

Now Vitt stood diagonal to her.

"Walk to me," she called out.

She did the same, avoiding some of the underbrush and trees, but staying in a relatively straight line to Vitt.

The two women met.

"You think the four markers lead to something in the center?" Vitt asked.

"I do. We need to be close to the line formed by the other two markers."

They readjusted their meeting spot, trying to intersect that imaginary line.

"This is it," Vitt said. "Or as close as we can get without string."

"Arnaut had no string."

She stared down at the ground. Hard. Solid. A layer of scree and soil above a rock base. Together they cleared off the surface with their boots. Vitt hustled back to where their backpacks were located and returned with them, finding a collapsible shovel and starting to scrape away.

Then she saw it.

A notch in the stone, extending in both directions along a roughly straight line. Not deep. But there. And noticeable. Vitt stopped her efforts and concentrated on the line, using the shovel blade to scrape i clean and reveal more.

A corner came into view.

She stared at Vitt and said, "That's not natural."

"No, it's not."

Chapter 19

BELÁNCOURT APPROACHED THE PROMONTORY FROM THE OPPOSITE SIDE that Simone and Vitt had used. The sun was slowly reaching its full burning height. He climbed the incline slow and careful, making no noise and finding cover as soon as he reached the top. He could see the two women as they moved through the trees and brush, hearing the excitement in their voices. Then he'd listened to digging and the shrill sound of a metal blade sliding across hard rock. He decided not to tempt fate and approach any closer. Instead, he'd wait to see what happened. He had no direct line of sight on Simone or Vitt, but they were in front of him, about fifty meters away, among the foliage.

He recalled listening to Simone years ago talk about the mythical Lake of Learning. She'd always believed that the Cathar who escaped Montségur was a messenger of God and that divine providence had guarded his every move. Proof of that conclusion was the fact that what he'd hidden away had remained hidden for eight centuries. Of course, few had ever really gone in search of it, and this whole place, for the past sixty years, had been a protected national park. A bit difficult to engage in a full-scale treasure hunting expedition. Yet Simone and Vitt were here, among the mountains and trees, zeroed in on one particular spot. Why? Had the Book of Hours truly revealed the Path to Light? Was the whole thing real?

He hoped so.

Because he'd derive no greater pleasure than in depriving Simone of its joy.

CASSIOPEIA STARED AT WHAT HER SHOVEL HAD REVEALED.

An indentation in the rock floor that formed an oblong-shaped square, about a meter wide on each side. She stamped her boot atop its center. Nothing moved. She tapped it with her shovel. No hollow sound. The indentation itself had long filled in and was more a shallow u-shaped groove in the rock than a true seam.

The Cathar version of X marks the spot?

"Is it a way down?" Simone asked.

An excellent question.

"This was an island. Once a big limestone rock sticking out of a lake." She glanced around at the mount. "It's possible that the way to go is down."

She'd anticipated the contingency that whatever they were after might be buried, particularly in a cave, as southern France was littered with them.

"Let's find out."

Inside her backpack Cassiopeia found the blasting caps she'd brought. At the castle site they were sometimes used to loosen stone at the quarry, one of the few violations of the only-tools-and-materials-from-the-past rule. She returned and used the shovel to chip away four small holes at the corners of the indentation. The caps came with their own detonators that were radio controlled. Not overly powerful explosives, but concentrated and quite effective. She slipped a cap into each hole and filled in the cavities with rock and soil.

"Let's get back," she said.

And they retreated twenty meters away, seeking cover behind a large boulder. She activated the transmitter and hoped there was nobody nearby to hear anything, especially one of the park rangers.

She pressed the button.

BELÁNCOURT FELT THE ROCK QUAKE UNDER HIS FEET AND DEBRIS FLEW out in every direction. He'd wondered what Vitt had been doing with all he digging.

Now he knew.

It took a few moments for the dust to settle. He was still on the ncline, near the crest, safe behind a cluster of rock, able to see what was happening. Vitt and Simone flitted in and out among the trees. He calmed his breathing, listened beyond his adrenaline, and approached where the explosion had occurred.

What was happening?

CASSIOPEIA STARED IN ASTONISHMENT AT THE HOLE IN THE GROUND.

The blasting caps had shattered the stone, which was apparently some sort of plug over an underground cavity, revealing a black yaw about three quarters of a meter in diameter. She bent down, lifted a small chunk of rock, and dropped it into the hole. It hit the ground a few seconds later.

"That's not all that deep," she said. "I brought rope."

She found a tight coil of thick nylon and tied one end to the nearest tree. She then tossed the rest into the hole. She'd brought along two flashlights.

"Let me go first," Simone said.

She was going to argue, but decided it would not do any good, so she simply nodded. Before Simone stepped into the hole, she shined her flashlight down. The bottom appeared about four meters below.

Simone slipped on a pair of thick leather gloves.

This woman had come prepared.

But who was she to judge?

She'd brought along her own gloves.

Simone sat on the edge of the opening and gripped the rope, working her way into the hole. It only took a few seconds for her to be on solid earth again.

"It's an easy drop," Simone called up.

She grabbed both backpacks and dropped them down.

Before descending, she scanned the surroundings one last time.

All seemed quiet.

Hopefully, it would stay that way.

BELÁNCOURT WATCHED AS CASSIOPEIA VITT DISAPPEARED INTO THE ground, following Simone. The explosion had apparently exposed a way down into the earth. There'd been some noise as the charges exploded, but nothing ear-shattering, unless someone had been really close by.

He debated what to do next.

Follow?

That could be a problem.

The confines below could be tight and, with only one way in and out, exposure could be an issue. But the time had come to repay Simone. She needed to feel the hurt and pain he'd felt all these past years. She had to know that there was a price to be paid for murder. Governments called it capital punishment. He saw it as simple retribution. Unfortunately, Cassiopeia Vitt found herself in the middle.

Not a good place.

But that was not his problem.

Chapter 20

CASSIOPEIA FOLLOWED SIMONE DOWN A NARROW FISSURE CUT through limestone that led away from the former-island toward the nearby cliff face. The dank and moldy air smelled of decay and slid across her skin as heavy as a towel. She wondered how long it had been since a human had walked here.

If ever.

Simone seemed unfazed and unafraid, plunging into the darkness, following the beam of her flashlight. For an academician this woman had spunk.

"Maybe we should slow down," she said.

She'd been in enough situations like this to know that an easy way in most times meant trouble. There could be boobytraps. Danger. But she told herself that this could be a Cathar site, and Cathars were not violent.

The tunnel ended at a gallery with four other openings out, like fingers from the palm of a hand.

Simone stopped.

Overhead the vault was studded with the mutilated stumps of stalactites, jarred free by disturbances in the ground, their remnants scattered across the floor as rock and gravel. Cassiopeia scanned the walls with her light and was stunned at what she saw.

She counted over fifty wall paintings.

Bison. Horses. Ponies. Faces.

She stepped close, bent down near the floor, and saw the outline of a little horse, barely five centimeters long, finely executed in a flat red tint with engraved outlines. Its careful technique and disproportionately long neck and slender limbs brought to mind other Paleolithic paintings she'd seen in other French and Spanish caves.

She studied three grotesque human forms, also painted in red outline on the concave wall of a little niche. The figure of a man, the head in profile, the rest of the body facing to the front. A ridge of rock formed an enormous vertical phallus. She smiled at the artist's ingenuity. The second was a silhouette outlined in black with rounded back and pendent arms. It had horns and a tail, bringing to mind a sorcerer. The third figure, surrounded by stalagmites, showed a long head with retreating forehead and projecting jaw. All of the images, human and animal, were reduced to their essential traits.

Simone seemed fascinated by the display too. "Isn't it odd how they so carefully drew animals, but were so careless with people?"

She agreed. "I've always thought them intentionally distorted. Mere masks of reality. I never believed that men who could draw animals in so masterly a fashion were incapable of doing the same with people."

"You've seen other paintings?"

"In several caves. Near Lascaux, Font-de-Gaume, Les Combarelles, and around Monte Castillo. This area is loaded with them."

All were evidence from tens of thousands of years ago, when Stone Age humans occupied the Pyrenees and left behind a record of their world. Some were monochrome, usually in black or red. While most were polychrome, drawing on several colors with a mixture of techniques. Some were engraved, made by cutting lines into the rock surface with a flint or tool. Others were mere sketches with charcoal or manganese.

"These are some of the best I've ever seen," she said to Simone. "Incredible. They've been here since prehistoric times, undisturbed."

"Except by the Cathars, who chose this as their vault."

The drip, drip of water, eerie like a half-human cry, continued to break the silence. From which offshoot it originated was hard to say.

"We need to focus on why we're here," Simone said. "Though these drawings are, indeed, a significant archeological find."

"Okay. What now?"

BELÁNCOURT USED THE ROPE TO DESCEND INTO THE BLACK HOLE, finding the bottom. A tunnel stretched ahead into blackness, not a thing visible beyond the light seeping down from above.

He reached beneath his jacket and found the gun that he'd brought along, safe in a shoulder holster. In France, to own a gun you first had to acquire a hunting or sporting license, which required a psychological evaluation. A pain, but necessary if you wanted to hunt. He'd managed to fool the examiner and was easily approved. Pistols and revolvers were not allowed ever, but that didn't stop people from carrying them. He'd owned several for years, along with his hunting rifles. Mainly for personal protection, since a man in his situation was susceptible to terrorists or kidnappers.

Or at least that's what he told people.

He gripped the gun in his left hand.

Then advanced ahead into the dense realm of blackness.

SIMONE TRIED TO CONTAIN HERSELF. SHE'D IMAGINED THIS MOMENT for a long time. Now she was here. Think. Answer Vitt's question.

What now?

With her light she surveyed the walls and the four other openings that led out.

And saw them.

Etched into limestone.

Four letters.

From the Cathar code.

"You see that?" she asked Vitt.

"I do. They're similar to what's in the manuscript, on the page that led us here."

She approached one of the etchings. Crude. Seemingly done in haste. Not totally complete, but enough for the letter to be clear. She reached into her pocket and found her phone. She'd recorded several images of the manuscript page.

Just in case.

Between the upside down doves and the words that translated to *lake* and *learning*, along the Path to Light, was one random symbol from the chart.

She glanced up at the walls.

And saw it.

To her right.

The same letter, marking one of the exits.

"It's down that way," she said. "It's the only thing that makes sense."

BELÁNCOURT STOOD IN THE BLACKNESS JUST BEFORE WHERE THE tunnel entered a large chamber, one where Simone and Vitt now stood. They both held flashlights and were studying the walls.

He listened to their conversation and to Simone's declaration of where they should head next. If they decided to retreat back his way they'd run right into him. His grip on the gun tightened as he watched them both, with packs shouldered to their backs, disappear into another tunnel, their lights fading to black. So far, he'd not used any light. Instead, he'd felt his way ahead in the darkness, using their lights in the distance as beacons. Now he stood in absolute blackness. To get across to where they'd gone he'd have to use some illumination.

So he found his phone.

And lit the screen.

Then followed.

Chapter 21

CASSIOPEIA EMERGED FROM THE TUNNEL RIGHT BEHIND SIMONE, AND they both stared up in amazement. They'd entered a large chamber, its walls pregnant with age and damp towering up thirty meters. The path to here had taken them down an incline, deeper into the ground, then through a natural stone archway. The chamber also accommodated water that entered on one side and exited on the other, confined to a channel, the stream's flow slow and steady and without a sound. If not for their flashlights, they would have never known the water was there.

There were no other exits.

"This can't be the end," Simone said.

"Don't forget," Cassiopeia said, "all this was set in motion over eight hundred years ago. What we're looking at might be entirely different from then. There's been a lot of geological change."

At the edge of the stream she shined her light into the water, then bent down, dipped a finger in, and brought it up to her nose. No odor. Probably clean from being filtered through the limestone. She was thirsty, but the bottled water in her pack was far safer to trust. No telling what long forgotten bacteria might lurk here.

She washed her light over the walls. More paintings came into view. A horse, bison, wild goat, and the curved, branched antlers of a reindeer.

Then she saw it.

Set apart. By itself. Much larger than the other images. A bison, painted in a flat red tint with the horns, spine, and tail outlined. More engraved lines emphasized details. Head down, feet thrust forward, back arched. It seemed to snort with rage and pain, thrilled with life.

"*Bèstia roja*," she said. "Now we know what those words meant in the manuscript. Red Beast. That's one of the largest drawings I've ever seen."

Her light also revealed that the stream bulged toward the image on the wall, forming a small lake, one that shimmered like a sheet of wrinkled tin foil.

Coincidence?

Or was that there eight hundred years ago?

She saw a niche in the limestone wall, about a meter up from the water. On it rested another religious casket, similar to the one that had come out of the ground. Shiny.

Golden.

SIMONE DROPPED TO HER KNEES AND PRAYED TO THE GOD OF GOOD, thanking Him for all His wisdom. She'd accomplished what no other *Perfecti* had managed. She'd found The Truth.

For I say that just as it is impossible for that which is past not to be in the past, so it is impossible for that which is in the future not to be in the future. This is especially true in God, who from the beginning understood and knew that which would come to pass, so that existence as something still to come was possible for an event before it occurred. God Himself is the sole cause of all causes, and above all if it is fact, as the opponents of truth assert, that God does whatever pleases Himself and His might is not affected by anyone.

Those sacred words had been proven true.

Once the Good Christians dominated all of southern France, winning the hearts and minds of the Languedoc. It had taken a genocidal and generation-long crusade to silence them. For centuries all the Cathars had of that past was the *Book of Two Principles*, the last surviving witness against orthodox theology. Seven sections long, about 35,000 words, written in the 13th century, but confiscated by the papists in the 14th century, where it remained until 1939, when it was finally published after six hundred years of suppression.

But was it authentic?

Had it been altered?

Nobody knew.

But here waited the Truth. Unaltered. Unchanged. Exactly as it had been when written. While the Cathar world crumbled, and they willingly died by the thousands, the Truth had lain right here, at the end of the Path to Light.

She stood from her prayer and decided not to remove her boots or socks or roll up her jeans. Just go. "I'll take a look."

She kept the backpack on and stepped into the water. Surely cold. No. Freezing. Thankfully it was little more than ankle deep and her boots offered some insulation.

The lake itself was more a giant puddle, about ten meters across to the other side where the great red bison waited. One hand held the flashlight which she kept pointed ahead, keeping a watch, making sure the water stayed shallow.

She slushed her way to the other side and stepped out.

In the niche, beneath the red bison, about chest high for her, rested another gold casket, similar, but a bit larger than the one found at Givors. She stepped close and saw that the top was encrusted with precious stones. There were also tiny crosses, chalices, miters, and scepters, all crafted of gold. Cabochon rubies and amethyst stones formed a small crown on top.

"This had to be stolen," she called out. "It looks Catholic. My guess is that they knew this was not the best place for wood or base metals. So they used a reliquary from a church, since gold lasts forever. Just like they did when they buried your manuscript."

"Open it," Vitt said.

She agreed, though the archeologist inside her said no. But this was not a scientific mission. Far from it. This was a quest.

She dropped the pack off her shoulders and laid the flashlight down in the niche. She noticed that the edges beneath the lid were sealed with what appeared to be wax. She found her pocket knife and scored the edges all the way around, the brittle wax chipping away in pieces. Then she gripped the two short sides of the lid with the palms of her hands and wiggled it free, lifting it off and setting it on the ground.

She grabbed the light and looked inside to see a thick pile of unbound vellum sheets. She carefully extracted them and saw line after line of writing. No colorful gilded illustrations. No fancy letters or beautiful calligraphy. Just ordinary script. Thoughts from centuries ago.

The Truth.

"What is it?" Vitt called out.

She read the opening words.

Since many persons are hampered in rightly understanding the truth, to enlighten them, to stimulate those who do have right understanding, and also for the delight of my soul, I have made it my purpose to explain our true faith by evidence from the Holy Scriptures and with eminently suitable arguments, invoking to my efforts the aid of the Father, of the Son, and of the Holy Spirit.

A chill swept through her.

"Our bible," she said.

CASSIOPEIA HEARD THE WORDS.

Our bible.

"Who are you?" she asked.

"I'm the senior *Perfecti* of the living Cathars. And this is our greatest treasure."

"You're the one who tried to steal the book, aren't you?"

"So many books and articles talk about the Cathar treasure in terms of gold and jewels. What a joke. It was never that. Instead"—and she motioned with the sheets—"these words are our treasure."

She noticed how her question had been ignored, yet answered.

"For Catholics and Protestants, the oldest Bible that exists anywhere in the world is from the 10th century," Simone said. "No one has a clue what the original text, written centuries before that, actually says. We only know what those who translated and interpreted it say it says. But here. Here we have the original words, preserved and kept safe for all time. A true treasure in every sense of the word."

Simone seemed entranced, gesturing with the sheets like a preacher from the pulpit, her voice rising and lowering in waves.

"We need to leave," Cassiopeia said, thinking it best to deal with the situation once they were back in fresh air.

"I don't think so," a male voice declared.

She whirled around.

Roland Beláncourt stood just beyond the tunnel entrance, holding a gun, aimed straight at her.

Chapter 22

CASSIOPEIA AIMED HER FLASHLIGHT TOWARD BELÁNCOURT AND SAW HIS face, alert with purpose, pinched with tension, his dark pupils darting back and forth like warning signals. He was not his usual perfect self. More like a man roused from sleep, hair ruffled, stubble on his chin.

"Lower that light," he said, motioning with the gun.

She did as told.

Across the shallow pond Simone stood, the pages in one hand, a flashlight in the other. Cassiopeia wanted to ask how he'd found them, why he was there, and more. But decided on a question that seemed to encompass it all. "What did she do to you?"

"She killed our child."

"Your marriage was childless."

Simone made a move. Beláncourt reacted and fired a shot that ricocheted off the limestone. The bang echoed off the chamber's tight confines and hurt her ears.

"Don't move again," he ordered.

Simone froze.

"We were childless," he said, his eyes watering. "She aborted the baby at twenty weeks."

She caught the shadow of sorrow in his face and began to understand what was happening here.

A clash of culture and religion.

"She decided, on her own, to do that," he added. "For her, bringing a child into this world would be cruel. Her insane God of Good would never want that."

His anger was growing with every word.

"She promised me she would not do any such thing. She told me that she wanted the child. But she lied."

"It was my right. My choice," Simone spit out. "Not yours. Mine alone."

He fired another shot her way that found more rock.

"No. It was not *your* choice. It was *our* choice. One you denied me."

"Why not have another?" she asked Beláncourt. "You annulled the marriage. Remarry."

"Unfortunately," he said, his voice barely a whisper, "after the marriage ended, I contracted chicken pox. A terrible case, late in life. I almost died. But I was rendered sterile by the experience."

"Your punishment," Simone said. "For the evil you inflicted on me. The evil of carrying a child. *Because I called and you did not answer. I spoke and you did not hear, and you did evil in my eyes, and you have chosen the things that displease me.*"

"Shut up," he yelled. "I hate your scriptures. I hate your religion. I. Hate. You."

SIMONE STOOD WITH THE TRUTH IN HER HAND.

Its presence gave her strength.

She noticed a few of the words on the top page, the writing in Occitan decipherable. *From this comes the basis for our service to God, in that we may fulfill His works, or rather, that God may consummate through us that which He proposes and wishes to be done.*

Another message?

But what was it He wished done?

BELÁNCOURT KEPT HIS ATTENTION ON BOTH WOMEN.

Simone was twenty meters away, across what appeared to be a shallow pond of water bulging from a stream that pierced the chamber. Vitt was much closer, a few meters to his left, in front of him.

Neither woman carried a weapon.

Both had flashlights.

He stepped a little farther into the chamber, the feeling of gnawing emptiness that he'd grown accustomed to there, in his stomach.

Fueling him.

"My dear ex-wife," he said with contempt in his voice, "decided that she wanted to be Cathar. *The one true* religion, she called it. She made that choice on her own and I went along. I did not interfere, recognizing that her beliefs were heartfelt and personal. Of course, I considered the whole thing a dead belief. Gone. Its concepts a thing of the past. But I was wrong."

"Yes, you were," Simone said. "We are far from dead. There are believers everywhere. Men and women who want to lead good lives. Who want to achieve everlasting happiness. Who have no need for a pope or bishops. I watch over them."

He looked at Vitt. "She's their *Perfecti*. Their priest. Their special one. That all happened after we split. She became much more fanatical."

"You watched her?" Vitt asked.

He nodded.

"Strange thing for a man to do who hates his ex-wife," Vitt said.

"Not at all. I've simply been waiting for this moment. True, I could have denied her many petty things. Some tiny disappointments." He shook his head. "But that would not have been as satisfying. I knew she was after the great Truth. I knew that a Book of Hours with a rose design on the cover could lead the way. So I waited for this moment, ready to deny what is most important to her."

"It won't replace that child," Vitt said.

SIMONE'S LIMBS TREMBLED WITH RAGE.

"You never understood a thing," she called out. "You thought that bringing a child into this world was something of joy. Of happiness. It's not. It's cruel to bring a child into this physical existence. Cruel to subject him or her to the evils that Satan tempts us with in this world. The joy only comes from leaving this hell. I saved our child that pain. He or she is now with the God of Good."

"You sucked our fetus from your womb," he said. "It was twenty

weeks old. Defined. A person. Alive. You slaughtered a living being.
You played God and decided who would live and die. You imposed your
idiocy on both me and that unborn child."

His voice cracked and she heard the same emotion that had passed
between them years ago when she told him how the pregnancy had
ended.

He'd thought it a miscarriage.

But she told him the truth.

"I will have those pages," he said. "Or by God I. Will. Kill. You."

CASSIOPEIA WAS BECOMING CONCERNED.

The situation was escalating out of control. A lot had passed
between these two, and what should have been a private matter for them
to resolve had now become a war in which she found herself, literally,
right in the middle, a hostile face on either side, both conveying silent
menace.

One armed.

The other not.

She should have brought a gun, but there'd been no indication of that
level of trouble. And traveling around France with a loaded, concealed
weapon was anything but legal. Not that laws necessarily were an issue
for her. They certainly weren't for Beláncourt.

"Do you need that gun?" she asked, staying calm. "We're not armed.
There's no threat here, except from you."

"The threat level depends on Simone's cooperation."

She was afraid of that.

SIMONE STARED DOWN AT THE BACKPACK ON THE GROUND, A METER OR
so from the water's edge.

She'd come prepared.

Her gun lay inside.

After the encounter in the cathedral she knew that Roland was not going to back away. He'd made his intentions clear, which was exactly why she'd risked the personal encounter inside the church. It was important she knew exactly what she was facing. And the visit had confirmed that her ex-husband was on the offensive. She'd known him for over twenty years. He'd not become a billionaire by being timid. He knew how to get what he wanted. Their last encounter, just before the annulment was granted, had been anything but amicable. His last words to her emphatic. *Someday, somehow, you will pay for what you did.*

But his words rang hollow then and now.

She was not afraid to die. Not in the least. But she was afraid to fail, and it was important that she escape this underground vault and bring The Truth back into the light.

Go with God, although He knew fully and foresaw from eternity the fate of all His angels. His wisdom and providence did not make His angels become demons. They became demons and things of evil by their own will, because they did not wish to remain holy and humble before their Lord. They wickedly puffed themselves up in pride against Him.

So true.

Now she knew what had to be done.

BELÁNCOURT AIMED HIS GUN TOWARD SIMONE. "COME OVER HERE and bring those pages."

His ex-wife did not obey.

Nothing new there.

Their marriage had battered itself to a standstill with plenty of cruel, blunt words. Toward the end they'd little more than shared space, the cursory enjoyment of each other fading to nothing. He knew of wives who wore away their husbands. Others who made a cockold—jealous, suspicious, agonized fools whose work suffered and reputations declined. Simone had gone to the farthest extreme and killed their baby.

Bad marriages, though, were seldom fatal.

Yet this was something altogether different.

A choking urgency enveloped him, sending electric spasms to his muscles and brain, urging action. He readjusted the gun's aim at Cassiopeia Vitt. "How about I shoot her first? Would you like that,

Simone? Does your precious Truth sanction you allowing someone else to die for your beliefs? Oh, I forgot. It actually does, since you killed our child. But this woman is not a child. Not a Cathar."

"You would kill her?" Simone asked.

"With no hesitation."

CASSIOPEIA COULD NOT DECIDE IF BELÁNCOURT WAS BLUFFING. Unfortunately, there was little she could do about any of it since she was totally exposed and unarmed. Neither was a good situation. So—

Be patient.

That's what Cotton would say.

Wait for your moment.

SIMONE STEELED HERSELF.

For one who knows fully all things that shall come to pass is powerless, in so far as He's self-consistent to do anything except that which He himself has known from eternity that He shall do.

She was meant to resurrect that which had been lost. Why else had the God of Good sent her along the path she'd taken the past decade? It all made sense. Especially now, with The Truth in hand. Only two things stood in her way.

Time to deal with the first.

"All right, Roland. I'm coming over."

She bent down to get her pack.

"Leave it," he called out.

"I'm placing these pages inside. I don't want anything to happen to them. If you don't like that, shoot me."

He hesitated, then said, "Okay. But slowly."

She opened the flap and slid the thick bundle in, hoping not to cause them any damage. Vellum was tough, but not invincible. The bundle projected from the top, not fully able to go inside. She switched off her light and set it inside the pack. Then she lifted the backpack and cradled t across her chest with both arms, her right hand near the open top.

The weight of defeat settled on her shoulders like a cloak.

But she shook it off.

Roland watched her from the shadows, visible in the penumbra of Vitt's flashlight. She took one step, then slipped her hand into the pack, gripped the gun, and fired across the water.

CASSIOPEIA SAW THE GUN AND HEARD THE SHOT AT THE SAME INSTANT. There was no time to avoid any of the consequences and she heard the bullet thud into Beláncourt's flesh.

He slumped over.

Simone fired again.

Beláncourt collapsed and smacked the floor hard, his gun clattering away. Cassiopeia realized her light was providing the target, so she extinguished the beam, plunging the chamber into darkness and blotting everything from sight.

Silence reigned.

Simone's light came back on. "Where are you?"

Cassiopeia sought cover behind a small clump of rocks away from the water's edge. Not all that tall, so she had to lie flat on the damp ground, hunching behind. What she needed was Beláncourt's gun. But she could not risk darting out in the open. Simone would spot her quickly with the flashlight. What would happen then was anybody's guess. Better to stay still and quiet.

Not a sound came from Beláncourt.

The situation was tight, but not dire. She'd found herself in worse before. Luckily, a weapon was within reach, but it would take some doing to get it.

The gleam of Simone's light jerked from one spot to another.

Searching.

"He's dead, Simone," she called out.

The light came her way and zeroed in. She stayed low, behind the rocks. To get her, Simone would have to come through the water, closer.

"He was aiming a gun at me. He threatened to kill me. I was entirely justified in protecting myself."

"Yes, you were. He made his intentions clear."

"But I don't hate him. It's wrong to hate anyone. He simply has no understanding of the things I do. We once loved each other. We were happy. Our marriage was good. He just could not understand the depth of my beliefs."

She decided to keep her talking. "Were you Cathar when you married?"

"No. It came later, as I obtained my doctorate and learned more and more about the Good Ones. Their message resonated with me. I became a devotee. Eventually, I received the *Consolamentum* from an older woman and became *Perfecti*. When she died, I became the senior *Perfecti*. I look after the others. They depend on me. I never intended on becoming pregnant. I took measures to ensure it would not happen. But it still did. It was the work of Satan. Part of what he does. It had to end. So I ended it."

"Why don't we leave here and call the police? I'll back up your claim of self-defense. You still have much work to do, and now you have The Truth."

SIMONE STOOD AT THE WATER'S EDGE AND STARED ACROSS THE DARK chamber at where Vitt had taken refuge. Just beyond the stream, ten meters away. The papist was dead. Good riddance. But what of Vitt? Was she an ally? Or an enemy? She sounded like the former. But could she take the chance of finding out?

One hand held the flashlight, the other the gun.

The backpack lay before her on the ground.

She recalled the words from The Truth.

From this comes the basis for our service to God, in that we may fulfill His works, or rather, that God may consummate through us that which He proposes and wishes to be done.

Her service seemed clear.

She said, "All right, let's leave and go to the police."

CASSIOPEIA WAS NO FOOL.

That concession came way too easy, especially from a person who'd just shot a man in cold blood. Sure, Beláncourt had a gun, but she'd now concluded that he was not going to use it, no matter how threatening he may have been. The man was a billionaire with a massive corporation. He was not going to throw all that away just to kill his ex-wife. He'd come to deprive her of having the manuscript, whether by taking or destroying it. No matter. There'd be no crime there.

Only satisfaction.

Simone, though, was a different matter. She was unhinged, and her offer that they leave and go to the police rang hollow. For someone so obviously competent in matters of history, it seemed inconceivable that he'd be so ill prepared here.

And she had not been.

The woman had come armed.

In the wash of the beam that swept over her, she spotted Beláncourt's gun about two meters away, exposed, out in the open, on the floor. She readied the flashlight in her left hand, thumb on the on/off switch.

Everything had to happen fast.

She switched on the light, aimed it up and over the rock toward Simone, its bright beam right in the other woman's eyes. Using that instant of confusion, she kept the light pointed and lunged to her right, toward the gun.

SIMONE WAS PARTIALLY BLINDED BY THE SEARING LIGHT BURNING HER eyes. Instinctively, she raised the hand holding the flashlight to block the incoming rays, the hand with the gun thrust forward.

Firing.

Toward the source of the problem.

CASSIOPEIA MOVED RIGHT, KEEPING THE LIGHT AIMED ACROSS THE shallow pond. Simone fired twice, but at her former position, not where she was now, two meters away with her hand gripping Beláncourt's weapon. Simone seemed to rebound from the momentary blindness, her light beam searching, then finding Cassiopeia.

But she was ready.

Gun aimed.

Trigger pulled.

The first shot caught Simone in the chest.

The second sent her down.

The other flashlight dropped away and rolled on the floor, finding the water, where it rested, partially submerged.

She'd not wanted to do that, but there'd been no choice.

She came to her feet and walked across the pond. Simone lay flat, her dead eyes boring up into the ceiling.

She shook her head.

"There was no need," she whispered. "None at all."

But reason had played little part in what had just happened.

Just action and reaction.

She reached down and closed Simone's eyes, hoping she'd found the God of Good. Then she lifted the backpack with the manuscript and returned to where Beláncourt lay dead. Murdered. She felt for him. He'd lost a child through no choice of his own. Which obviously changed his life.

And not for the better.

Neither he nor Simone had been willing to concede a thing.

A sadness filled the quiet.

One that signaled forgiveness?

Probably not.

Killing someone came with repercussions, one she'd feel in the days ahead, though there'd been no choice. She should use the rest of her blasting caps and seal them both here for eternity. But that would not be smart. A man like Beláncourt would be missed. People would come looking. Questions asked. Better to deal with what happened head on. She wondered though if anyone would miss Simone Forte. Would the believers? If so, who would look after them?

Hard to say.

But a part of her genuinely hoped that someone would.

Writer's Note

This story deals with a fascinating area of the world (the Languedoc region of southern France), a fascinating time period (the 13th century), and a fascinating religion (Catharism). Steve set his novel *The Templar Legacy* there in 2006. M.J. used the locale for the more recent *The Library of Light and Shadows* (2017). Steve has visited the region several times. M.J. spends a month there every summer.

Time now to separate fact from fiction.

Cassiopeia's authentic castle rebuilding (chapter 1) is based on an actual project located near Treigny, France. It's called Guédelon Castle, described as an exercise in *experimental archaeology*. Only period construction techniques, tools, and costumes are utilized. All of the materials, including the wood and stone, are obtained locally. Its design is according to an architectural model developed during the 12th and 13th centuries by Philip II of France. In real life, construction has been ongoing since 1997.

Books of Hours (chapter 1) exist and were indeed the medieval equivalent of today's coffee table tomes. Bright, vibrant, and full of illustration, they deservedly earned the title *illuminated manuscript*. All of their history and details as described in the story are accurate. The main difference is that ours is written in Occitan, the then-language of southern France, as opposed to Latin, the usual choice.

The Occitan Cross (chapter 1, and the art used at the point of view breaks) is today many times called the Cathar Cross. That's a mistake. The Cathars rejected all religious symbolism and would have had no need for a cross. Today it is used as the symbol of Occitania, a cultural area that includes the southern third of France, part of Spain, Monaco, and areas of Italy. About sixteen million people live in the region, but only a small portion are proficient in Occitan. In this story, all of the references from the Book of Hours and The Truth are in Occitan.

The two gold religious caskets (chapters 1 and 21) are based on actual artifacts that would have been present in Catholic churches. Considering hostilities that existed at the time, it would not have been unusual for Cathars to appropriate two of them for use.

The Lake of Learning in this story is our creation. But there is a real

Lake of Learning located in Ireland's Killarney National Park. Lough Leane, from the Irish Loch Léin, means "lake of learning." It's the northernmost of the three lakes there, the largest body of fresh water in the region. That lake is dotted with several forested islands, including Innisfallen, which holds the remains of a ruined abbey. The monks who once lived there were charged with teaching and learning, hence how the lake acquired its name. Steve visited the ruins and was inspired enough that he and M.J. created their own in France.

Several actual French locales were utilized. Aerospace Valley outside Toulouse is there (chapter 6). Carcassonne (chapters 14 and 15) is a world treasure. Everything noted in the story associated with that ancient city—the walls, shops, castle, and hotel—exists, including the torture museum. Mirepoix (chapter 12) is another medieval gem, its main square something to see. The Cathédrale Saint-Étienne in Toulouse (chapter 16) is indeed an odd mix of architecture and style. Then there are the Pyrenees themselves (chapter 18). Massive, mysterious, and mythical. A mountain range like no other in the world.

Montségur is a special locale (chapter 9). It was the place of the Cathars' last great stand, one that ended in surrender and sacrifice. Everything in the story from there is faithfully recorded. The climb up is tough, arduous, and not without danger. The climb down even more precarious (Steve did it). The monument standing at the base of the *pog*, commemorating the lives lost on March 16, 1244, appears on the cover. There is indeed a sheer cliff face on one side, and a persistent legend is that one or more of the Cathars escaped down its side. *The Story of Arnaut*, though, is our invention.

The alphabet noted in chapter 17 is called Enochian, a language recorded in the private journals of the Englishman John Dee in the late 16th century. Dee claimed that the language had been revealed to him by angels. The term "Enochian" comes from Dee's belief that the biblical patriarch Enoch had been the last human (before him) to know the language. In any event, it worked well here as a Cathar code.

The cave paintings that appear in chapters 20 and 21 exist in caves all across southern France. They are incredible wonders from tens of thousands of years ago, the "books" of that era, as images were the only way they had to memorialize thoughts.

This novella deals heavily with the Cathar religion. Both Steve and M.J. have wanted to utilize it in a story. It flourished for a long time, reaching its peak in the 13th century, when it became a direct threat to Rome and the Catholic Church. The Albigensian Crusade was the first time Christians were sent to kill other Christians, and tens of thousands were slaughtered, the Cathar religion wiped out. The pledge to the crusaders of forgiveness of all their sins (chapter 3), including the murder of fellow Christians if they participated, is real. Catharism was overseen by a select group of believers who rose to the level of Perfect. They are labeled differently depending on the texts you read. Sometimes Perfect, other times Parfait, occasionally *Perfecti*. We chose the latter.

The *Melhoramentum and Consolamentum* rituals described in Chapter 8 are authentic. The prayers and sequence of the ceremony are likewise correct. The winged dove (chapter 14) is one image the Cathars seemed to embrace, as it represented freedom. It can be found carved all over the Languedoc. All of the italicized prayers that the *Perfecti* (Simone Forte) utters come from the Cathar document known as the *Book of Two Principles,* which is the largest and most complete Cathar teaching that has survived. Sadly, as noted in the story, both the Cathars and their writings were systematically destroyed.

Our document, The Truth, *La Vertat,* is fictional. But, who knows, somewhere across Occitania there may be a manuscript hidden away that survived the purge. A trove of original Cathar thought, unfiltered and unaffected by subsequent interlopers. One that explains the religion in precise detail.

And, who knows, perhaps the words of Guilhèm Belibaste, the last *Perfecti* burned at the stake in 1321, may still come to pass.

Al cap dels set cent ans, verdajara lo laurel.

The laurel will flourish again in 700 years.

Also from M.J. Rose and Steve Berry

The Museum of Mysteries
A Cassiopeia Vitt Adventure
By Steve Berry and M.J. Rose
Now available!

Cassiopeia Vitt takes center stage in this exciting novella from New York Times bestsellers M.J. Rose and Steve Berry.

In the French mountain village of Eze, Cassiopeia visits an old friend who owns and operates the fabled Museum of Mysteries, a secretive place of the odd and arcane. When a robbery occurs at the museum, Cassiopeia gives chase to the thief and is plunged into a firestorm.

Through a mix of modern day intrigue and ancient alchemy, Cassiopeia is propelled back and forth through time, the inexplicable journeys leading her into a hotly contested French presidential election. Both candidates harbor secrets they would prefer to keep quiet, but an ancient potion could make that impossible. With intrigue that begins in southern France and ends in a chase across the streets of Paris, this magical, fast-paced, hold-your-breath thriller is all you've come to expect from M.J. Rose and Steve Berry.

About the Authors

Steve Berry

STEVE BERRY is the New York Times and #1 internationally bestselling author of fourteen Cotton Malone novels and four stand alones. He has 25 million books in print, translated into 40 languages. With his wife, Elizabeth, he is the founder of History Matters, which is dedicated to historical preservation. He serves as an emeritus member on the Smithsonian Libraries Advisory Board and was a founding member of International Thriller Writers, formerly serving as its co-president.
To learn more visit www.SteveBerry.org.

M.J. Rose

New York Times bestseller, M.J. Rose grew up in New York City mostly in the labyrinthine galleries of the Metropolitan Museum, the dark tunnels and lush gardens of Central Park and reading her mother's favorite books before she was allowed. She believes mystery and magic are all around us but we are too often too busy to notice... books that exaggerate mystery and magic draw attention to it and remind us to look for it and revel in it.
Please visit her blog, Museum of Mysteries at http://www.mjrose.com/blog/
Rose's work has appeared in many magazines including *Oprah* magazine and she has been featured in the *New York Times, Newsweek, Wall Street Journal, Time, USA Today* and on the Today Show, and NPR radio. Rose graduated from Syracuse University, spent the '80s in advertising, has a commercial in the Museum of Modern Art in New York City and since 2005 has run the first marketing company for authors - Authorbuzz.com
Rose lives in Connecticut with her husband, the musician and composer Doug Scofield.

The Malta Exchange
A Cotton Malone Novel
By Steve Berry
Now Available

A deadly race for the Vatican's oldest secret fuels *New York Time.*
bestseller Steve Berry's latest international Cotton Malone thriller.

The pope is dead. A conclave to select his replacement is about to
begin. Cardinals are beginning to arrive at the Vatican, but one has fled
Rome for Malta in search of a document that dates back to the 4th
century and Constantine the Great.

Former Justice Department operative, Cotton Malone, is at Lake
Como, Italy, on the trail of legendary letters between Winston Churchill
and Benito Mussolini that disappeared in 1945 and could re-write history.
But someone else seems to be after the same letters and, when Malone
obtains then loses them, he's plunged into a hunt that draws the attention
of the legendary Knights of Malta.

The knights have existed for over nine hundred years, the only
warrior-monks to survive into modern times. Now they are a global
humanitarian organization, but within their ranks lurks trouble — the
Secreti— an ancient sect intent on affecting the coming papal conclave
With the help of Magellan Billet agent Luke Daniels, Malone races the
rogue cardinal, the knights, the *Secreti*, and the clock to find what has been
lost for centuries. The final confrontation culminates behind the walls of
the Vatican where the election of the next pope hangs in the balance.

* * * *

Here's an excerpt:

Chapter One
Tuesday, May 9
Lake Como, Italy
8:40 A.M.

COTTON MALONE STUDIED THE EXECUTION SITE.
A little after 4:00 P.M., on the afternoon of April 28, 1945, Benito

Mussolini and his mistress, Claretta Petacci, were gunned down just a few feet away from where he stood. In the decades since, the entrance to the Villa Belmonte, beside a narrow road that rose steeply from Azzano about a half a mile below, had evolved into a shrine. The iron gate, the low wall, even the clipped hedges were still there, the only change from then was a wooden cross tacked to the stone on one side of the gate that denoted Mussolini's name and date of death. On the other side he saw another addition—a small, glass-fronted wooden box that displayed pictures of Mussolini and Claretta. A huge wreath of fresh flowers hung from the iron fence above the cross. Its banner read *egli vivra per sempre nel suore del suo popolo.*

He will always live in the hearts of people.

Down in the village he'd been told where to find the spot and that loyalists continued to venerate the site. Which was amazing, considering Mussolini's brutal reputation and that so many decades had passed since his death.

What a quandary Mussolini had faced.

Italy languishing in a state of flux. The Germans fast retreating. Partisans flooding down from the hills. The Allies driving hard from the south, liberating town after town. Only the north, and Switzerland, had offered the possibility of a refuge.

Which never happened.

He stood in the cool of a lovely spring morning.

Yesterday, he'd taken an afternoon flight from Copenhagen to the Milan-Malpensa Airport, then driven a rented Alfa Romeo north to Lake Como. He'd splurged on the sports car, since who didn't like driving a 237 horsepowered engine that could go from zero to sixty in four seconds. He'd visited Como before, staying at the stunning Villa d'Este during an undercover mission years ago for the Magellan Billet. One of the finest hotels in the world. This time the accommodations would not be anywhere near as opulent. He was on special assignment for British intelligence, working freelance, his target an Italian, a local antiques dealer who'd recently crept onto MI6's radar. Originally his job had been a simple buy and sell. Being in the rare book business provided him with a certain expertise in negotiating for old and endangered writings. But new information obtained last night had zeroed in on a possible hiding place, so the task had been modified. If the information proved correct, his orders were now to steal the items.

He knew the drill.

Buying involved way too many trails and, until yesterday, had been MI6's only option. But if what they wanted could be appropriated without paying for it, then that was the smart play. Especially considering that what they were after did not belong to the Italian.

He had no illusions.

Twelve years with the Magellan Billet, and a few more after that working freelance for various intelligence agencies, had taught him many lessons. Here, he knew he was being paid to handle a job *and* take the fall if anything went wrong. Which was incentive enough to not make any mistakes.

The whole thing, though, seemed intriguing.

In August 1945 Winston Churchill had arrived in Milan under the cover name of Colonel Warden. Supposedly, he'd decided to vacation along the shores of Lakes Como, Garda, and Lugano. Not necessarily a bad decision since people had been coming to the crystalized Alpine waters for centuries. The use of a code name ensured a measure of privacy but, by then, Churchill was no longer Britain's prime minister, having been unceremoniously defeated at the polls.

His first stop was the cemetery in Milan where Mussolini had been hastily buried. He'd stood at the grave, hat in hand, for several minutes. Strange considering the deceased had been a brutal dictator and a war enemy. He'd then traveled north to Como, taking up residence at a lakeside villa. Over the next few weeks the locals spotted him out gardening, fishing, and painting. No one at the time gave it much thought, but decades later historians began to look hard at the journey. Of course, British intelligence had long known what Churchill was after.

Letters.

Between him and Mussolini.

They'd been lost at the time of Mussolini's capture. Part of a cache of documents in two satchels that were never seen after April 27, 1945. Rumors were the local partisans had confiscated them. Some say they were turned over to the communists. Others pointed to the Germans. One line of thought proclaimed that they had been buried in the garden of the villa Churchill had rented.

Nobody knew anything for sure.

But something in August 1945 had warranted the personal intervention of Winston Churchill himself.

Cotton climbed back into the Alfa Romeo and continued his drive up the steep road. The villa where Mussolini and his mistress had spent their last night still stood somewhere nearby. He'd read the many conflicting accounts of what happened on that fateful Saturday. Details still eluded historians. In particular, the name of the executioner had been clouded by time. Several ultimately claimed the honor, but no one knew for sure who'd pulled the trigger. Even more mysterious was what happened to the gold, jewels, currency and documents Mussolini had intended to take to Switzerland. Most agree that a portion of the wealth had been dumped into the lake, as local fishermen later found gold there after the war. But, like with the documents, no meaningful cache had ever come to light. Until two weeks ago, when an e-mail arrived at the British embassy in Rome with an image of a scanned letter.

From Churchill to Mussolini.

More communications followed, along with four more images. No sale price had been arrived at for the five. Instead, Cotton was being paid 50,000 euros for the trip to Como, his negotiating abilities, and the safe return of all five letters.

The villa he was after sat high on a ridge, just off the road that continued on to the Swiss border about six miles away. All around him rose forests where partisans had hid during the war, waging a relentless guerilla campaign on both the Fascists and Germans. Their exploits were legendary, capped by the unexpected triumph in capturing Mussolini himself.

For Italy, World War II ended right here.

He found the villa, a modest three-storied rectangle, its stone stained with mold and topped by a pitched slate roof set among tall trees. Its many windows caught the full glare of the early morning sun, the yellow limestone seeming to drain of color as it basked in the bright light. Two white, porcelain greyhounds flanked the main entrance. Cypress trees dotted a well-kept yard along with topiary, both of which seemed mandatory for houses around Lake Como.

He parked in front and climbed out to a deep quiet.

The foothills kept rising behind the villa where the road continued its twisted ascent. To the east, through more trees sprouting spring flecks of green, he caught the dark blue stain of the lake, perhaps a half mile away and a quarter of that below. Boats moved silently back and forth across its mirrored surface. The air was noticeably cooler and, from the nearby garden, he caught a waft of wisteria.

He turned to the front door and came alert.

The thick wooden panel hung partially open.

White gravel crunched beneath his feet as he crossed the drive and stopped short of entering. He gave the door a little push and swung it open, staying on his side of the threshold. No electronic alarms went off inside. Nobody appeared. But he immediately saw a body sprawled across the terrazzo, face down, a crimson stain oozing from one side.

He carried no weapon. His intel had said that the house should be empty, its owner away until the late afternoon. MI6 had not only traced the e-mails it had received, but they'd also managed to compose a quick dossier on the potential seller. Nothing about him signaled a threat.

He entered and checked the body for a pulse.

None.

He looked around.

The rooms were pleasant and spacious, the papered walls ornamented with huge oil paintings, dark with age. Smells of musty flowers, candle wax, and tobacco floated in the air. He noticed a large walnut desk, rosewood melodeon, silk brocade sofas and chairs. Intricate inlaid armoires with glass fronts pressed the walls, one after the other, each loaded with objects on display like a museum.

But the place was in a shambles.

Drawers were half opened, tilted at crazy angles, shelves in disarray, a few of the armoires shattered, chairs turned upside down flung to the floor, some slashed and torn. Even some of the drapes had been pulled from their hangings and lay in crumpled heaps.

Somebody had been looking for something.

Nothing broke the silence save a parrot in a gilded cage that had once stood on a marble pedestal. Now the cage lay on the floor, battered and smashed, the pedestal overturned, the bird uttering loud, excited screeches.

He rolled the body over and noticed two bullet wounds. The victim was in his mid-to-late forties, with dark hair and a clean-shaven face. The villa's owner was about the same age, but this corpse did not match the description he'd been given.

Something clattered.

Hard and loud.

From above.

Then heavy footsteps.

Somebody was still here.

The hiding place he sought was located on the third floor, so he headed for the staircase and climbed, passing the second floor landing. A carpet runner lined the stone risers and cushioned his leather soles allowing no sound to betray his movement. At the third floor he heard more commotion, like a heavy piece of furniture slamming the floor. Whoever was searching seemed oblivious to any interruption.

He decided on a quick peek to assess things.

He crept ahead.

A narrow green runner ran down the center of the corridor's wood floor. At the far end, a half-opened window allowed in the morning sun and a breeze. He came to the room where the noise originated, which was the same room he'd been directed to find. Whoever had beat him here was well informed. He stopped at the open doorway and risked a quick glance.

And saw a stout bear.

Several hundred pounds, at least.

The source of the crash was evident from an armoire that lay overturned. The animal was exploring, swiping odds and ends off the tables, smelling everything as it clattered down. It stood facing away, toward one of the two half open windows.

He needed to leave.

The bear stopped its foraging and raised its head, sniffing.

Not good.

The animal caught his scent, turned, and faced him, snorting a growl.

He had a split second to make a decision.

Normally, you dealt with bears by standing your ground, facing them down. But that advice had clearly been offered by people who'd never been this close to one. Should he head back toward the stairs? Or dart into the room across the hall? One mistake on the way down to the ground floor and the bear would overtake him. He opted for the room across the hall and darted left, entering just as the animal rushed forward in a fit of speed surprising for its size. He slammed the door shut and stood inside a small bedroom, a huge porcelain stove filling one corner. Two more windows, half open, lined the outer wall, which faced the back of the villa.

He needed a second to think.

But the bear had other ideas.

The door crashed inward.

He rushed to one of the windows and glanced out. The drop down was a good thirty feet. That was at least a sprained ankle, maybe a broken bone or worse. The bear hesitated in the doorway, then roared.

Which sealed the deal.

He noticed a ledge just below the window. About eight inches wide. Enough to stand on. Out he went, flattening his hands against the warm stone, his spine pressed to the house. The bear charged the window, poking its head out, swiping a paw armed with sharp claws. He edged his way to the left and maneuvered himself out of range.

He doubted the animal was going to climb out.

But that didn't solve his problem.

What to do next.

Tiffany Blues

By MJ Rose

Now Available

The *New York Times* bestselling author of *The Library of Light and Shadow* crafts a dazzling Jazz Age jewel—a novel of ambition, betrayal, and passion about a young painter whose traumatic past threatens to derail her career at a prestigious summer artists' colony run by Louis Comfort Tiffany of Tiffany & Co. fame. "[M.J. Rose] transports the reader into the past better than a time machine could accomplish" (*The Associated Press*).

New York, 1924. Twenty-four-year-old Jenny Bell is one of a dozen burgeoning artists invited to Louis Comfort Tiffany's prestigious artists' colony. Gifted and determined, Jenny vows to avoid distractions and romantic entanglements and take full advantage of the many wonders to be found at Laurelton Hall.

But Jenny's past has followed her to Long Island. Images of her beloved mother, her hard-hearted stepfather, waterfalls, and murder, and the dank hallways of Canada's notorious Andrew Mercer Reformatory for Women overwhelm Jenny's thoughts, even as she is inextricably drawn to Oliver, Tiffany's charismatic grandson.

As the summer shimmers on, and the competition between the artists grows fierce as they vie for a spot at Tiffany's New York gallery, a series of suspicious and disturbing occurrences suggest someone knows enough about Jenny's childhood trauma to expose her.

Supported by her closest friend Minx Deering, a seemingly carefree socialite yet dedicated sculptor, and Oliver, Jenny pushes her demons aside. Between stolen kisses and stolen jewels, the champagne flows and the jazz plays on until one moonless night when Jenny's past and present are thrown together in a desperate moment, that will threaten her promising future, her love, her friendships, and her very life.

* * * *

Here's an excerpt:

Prologue
March 13, 1957
Laurelton Hall, Laurel Hollow
Oyster Bay, New York

I LOST MY HEART LONG BEFORE THIS FIRE DARKENED ITS EDGES. I WAS twenty-four years old that once-upon-a-time summer when I fell in love. A love that opened a door into a new world. A profusion of greens, shades of purples, spectrums of yellows, oranges, reds, and blues—oh, so many variations of blues.

I never dreamed I'd come back to Laurelton Hall, but I always trusted it would be there if I ever could visit. Now that will be impossible. For all that is left of that arcadia is this smoldering, stinking mess.

Somewhere in this rubble of charred trees, smashed tiles, and broken glass is my bracelet with its heart-shaped diamond and benitoite charm. Did my heart burn along with the magical house, the primeval forest, the lush bushes, and the glorious flowers? I'm not sure. Platinum is a hard metal. Diamonds are harder still. Or did just the engraving melt? And what of the man whose hand had grabbed at the bracelet? His muscle and flesh would have rotted by now. But what of the bones? Do bones burn? Back when it all happened, no report about a missing artist was ever made.

I take a few tentative steps closer to the rubble of the house. Bits of glass glint in the sun. A shard of ruby flashes, another of deep amethyst. I bend and pick up a fragment the size of my hand and wipe the soot off its surface.

With a start, I recognize this pattern.

Patterns, Mr. Tiffany once said, be they found in events, in nature, even in the stars in the firmament, are proof of history repeating itself. If we see randomness, it is only because we don't yet recognize the pattern.

So it shouldn't surprise me that of all the possible patterns, this is the one I've found. This remnant of the stained-glass clematis windows from Oliver's room. I remember how the light filtered through those windows, radiating color like the gems Mr. Tiffany used in his jewelry. How we stood in that living light and kissed, and the world opened up for me like an oyster, offering one perfect, luminous pearl. How that kiss became one more, then a hundred more. How we discovered each other's tastes and scents. How we shared that alchemical reaction when our passions ignited, combusted, and exploded, changing both of us forever.

Clutching the precious memory, I continue walking through the hulking mass of wreckage, treading carefully on the broken treasures. I listen for the familiar sounds—birds chirping, water splashing in the many fountains, and the endless rushing of the man-made waterfall that I always went out of my way to avoid.

But everything here is silent. Not even the birds have returned yet.

I learned about the fire seven days ago. I was at home in Paris, having breakfast, eating a croissant, drinking a café crème, and reading the *International*
Herald Tribune. The headline popped out at me like the obituary of an old friend with whom I had long been out of touch.

Old Tiffany Mansion Burns

An eight-level structure with twenty-five baths, the house was owned originally by the late Louis Comfort Tiffany of the jewelry firm that bears his name. At one time the estate covered 1,500 acres of woodland and waterfront.

I didn't realize my hand was shaking until I saw a splotch of coffee soak into my white tablecloth.

The structure later housed the Tiffany Art Foundation, which operated a summer school for artists.

The reporter wrote that a neighbor out walking his dog noticed flames coming from the clock tower of Laurelton's main house. Within hours, the mansion was ablaze. Fire companies came from as far as Hicksville and Glen Cove. Firemen drained all the neighboring swimming pools using the water to try to contain the conflagration. They carried hoses a half mile down to the Long Island Sound to siphon off that water, too. At one point, 435 firemen worked on the blaze, but the fire raged on and on for five days, defeating them. Those who lived nearby said the skies blackened as metal and wood, foliage, ephemera, and fabric burned.

The sky here is no longer black. But the smell of the fire persists. And no wonder, considering it burned for so long.

Once the present turns to past, all we have left are memories. Yes sometimes we can stand where we stood, see our ghost selves, and relive moments of our life. See the shadow of the man we loved. Of the friend we cherished. Of the mentor who made all the difference. Our memories turn specific. The terrier that played by the shoreline, joyously running in the sand. We can remember the smell of the roses. Look at the azure water and see the glimmer of the sun on the opposite shore and hear a fleeting few bars of jazz still lingering in the air.

If you were the only girl in the world . . . Staring into the remains of what is left, I see ghosts of the gardens and woods, the gazebo, terraces, rooms ablaze with stained glass—everywhere we walked and talked and kissed and cried. With my eyes closed, I see it all in my mind, but when I open them, all of it is gone, up in flames.

Mr. Tiffany once told me that there is beauty even in broken things. Looking back, there is no question I would not be the artist I am if not for that lesson. But would he be able to salvage any beauty out of this destruction?

No, I never dreamed I'd come back to Laurelton Hall. The Xanadu where I came of age as both a woman and a painter. Where I found my heart's desire and my palette's power. Where depravity bloomed alongside beds and fields of flowers, where creativity and evil flowed with the water in the many fountains. Where the sun shone on the tranquil sea and the pool's treacherous rock crystals reflected rainbows onto the stone patio. Where the glorious light streaming from Mr. Tiffany's majestic stained glass illuminated the very deep darkness that had permeated my soul and lifted me out of despair. And where I found the love that sustained me and remained in my heart even after Oliver and I parted.

Standing here, smelling the acrid stench, looking at the felled trees with their charcoal bark, the carbon-coated stones and bent metal frames that once held the master's windows, at the smoky, melting mess that was one of the greatest mansions on Long Island's Gold Coast, I know I never will see it again, not how it was that magical and awful summer of 1924.

The fire is still hot in spots, and a tree branch snaps. My reverie is broken. Leaves rustle. Rubble falls. Glass crushes. Twigs crack. Then comes a whisper.

Jenny.

But it can't be. The wind howling through a hollow tree trunk is playing a trick. Fooling me into thinking I am hearing his sapphire voice, its deep velvet tone.

As I listen to the repeated whisper—*Jenny*—I raise my hand to wipe at my tears and tell myself that it is the smoldering ash making my eyes water. The charms on my bracelet jingle as I lower my arm. And again the whisper…and again my name—*Jenny.*

~Special Thanks~

Doug Scofield
Kim Guidroz
Jillian Stein
Social Butterfly
Asha Hossain
Chris Graham
Kasi Alexander
Jessica Johns
Dylan Stockton
Simon Lipskar

Made in the USA
Coppell, TX
21 June 2020